THE PERFUME OF THE GODS

*By Barbara Cartland and published by
New English Library*

LOVE IN THE MOON
ENCHANTED
COUNT THE STARS
LOVE RULES
KNEEL FOR MERCY
FROM HATE TO LOVE
LIGHTS, LAUGHTER AND A LADY
BRIDE TO A BRIGAND
THERESA AND A TIGER
THE PERIL AND THE PRINCE
THE DEVILISH DECEPTION
NEVER FORGET LOVE
THE PERFUME OF THE GODS

THE PERFUME OF THE GODS

Barbara Cartland

NEW ENGLISH LIBRARY

Copyright © 1987 by Barbara Cartland

First published in Great Britain in 1987 by New English Library, Mill Road, Dunton Green, Sevenoaks, Kent. Editorial office: 47 Bedford Square, London WC1B 3DP.

All rights reserved. No part of this publication may be reproduced or transmitted in any form or by any means, electronically or mechanically, including photocopying, recording or any information storage or retrieval system, without either the prior permission in writing from the publisher or a licence, permitting restricted copying, issued by the Copyright Licensing Agency, 7 Ridgmount Street, London WC1E 7AE.

Typeset by Chippendale Type, Otley, West Yorkshire. Printed in Great Britain by Biddles Ltd., Guildford and Kings Lynn.

British Library Cataloguing in Publication Data

Cartland, Barbara
   The perfume of the gods
   I. Title
   823'.912[F]   PR6005.A765

ISBN 0-450-41284-9

THE PERFUME OF THE GODS

THE MARQUIS of Anglestone is shocked and horrified when Lady Hester Wynn, with whom he had a fiery *affaire de coeur* four months earlier, informs him that she is having a baby and intends to say that he is the father.

She admits that the real father is too poor to give her child the position he would have as the Marquis's child, and she threatens that if the Marquis does not agree to her outrageous suggestion, she will go to the Queen.

Shocked and appalled, the Marquis goes to his Club and on the spur of the moment finds a way of escape by taking a wager that he will enter the forbidden Moslem City of Mecca in disguise.

The Marquis journeys first to Egypt where he is helped by the famous explorer Sir Richard Burton, and then goes on to an obscure port in Southern Arabia, and is given a guide, an intelligent young Arab known as 'Ali'.

How the Marquis and Ali set off for Mecca and on the way, in the Capital of the Queen of Sheba's land, find a priceless treasure; how Ali's secret is discovered by the Marquis and how eventually he finds his Mecca is told in this unusual and fascinating 410th book by Barbara Cartland.

ABOUT THE AUTHOR

BARBARA CARTLAND, the world's most famous romantic novelist, who is also an historian, playwright, lecturer, political speaker and television personality, has now written over 450 books and sold over 450 million books all over the world.

She has also had many historical works published and has written four autobiographies as well as the biographies of her mother and that of her brother, Ronald Cartland, who was the first member of Parliament to be killed in the last war. This book has a preface by Sir Winston Churchill and has just been republished with an introduction by Sir Arthur Bryant.

'Love at the Helm', a novel written with the help and inspiration of the late Earl Mountbatten of Burma, Great Uncle of His Royal Highness The Prince of Wales, is being sold for the Mountbatten Memorial Trust.

Miss Cartland in 1978 sang an Album of Love Songs with the Royal Philharmonic Orchestra.

In 1976 by writing twenty-one books, she broke the world record and has continued for the following nine years with 24, 20, 23, 24, 24, 25, 22, 26, and 25. In the Guinness Book of Records she is listed as the world's top-selling author.

In private life Barbara Cartland, who is a Dame of Grace of the Order of St. John of Jerusalem, Chairman of the St. John Council of Hertfordshire and Deputy President of the St. John Ambulance Brigade, has fought for better conditions and salaries for Midwives and Nurses.

She has championed the cause for old people, had the law altered regarding gypsies and founded the first Romany Gypsy Camp in the world.

Barbara Cartland is deeply interested in Vitamin Therapy, and is President of the National Association for Health.

Her designs 'Decorating with Love' are being sold all over the U.S.A. and the National Home Fashions League made her in 1981, 'Woman of Achievement'.

Barbara Cartland's book 'Getting Older, Growing Younger', and her cookery book 'The Romance of Food' have been published in Great Britain, the U.S.A., and in other parts of the world.

She has also written a Children's Pop-Up Book entitled 'Princess to the Rescue'.

In 1984 she received at Kennedy Airport, America's Bishop Wright Air Industry Award for her contribution to the development of aviation when in 1931 she and two R.A.F. Officers thought of, and carried, the first aeroplane-towed glider air-mail.

An experiment is taking place with Mrs. Cartland at the moment which has never happened with any author before.

Eagle Moss (Patrick Cavendish) is bringing out a hardback book every fortnight at £1.95p. Beautifully bound in red and gold leather it will make a Barbara Cartland Library.

Other Books by Barbara Cartland

Romantic Novels, over 400, the most recently published being:

Bewildered in Berlin
Wanted – A Wedding Ring
The Earl Escapes
Starlight Over Tunis
The Love Puzzle
Love and Kisses
Sapphires in Siam
A Caretaker of Love
Secrets of the Heart
Riding to the Sky
The Dream and the Glory
(In aid of the St. John Ambulance Brigade)

Lovers in Lisbon
Love is Invincible
The Goddess of Love
An Adventure of Love
A Herb for Happiness
Only a Dream
Saved by Love
Little Tongues of Fire
A Chieftain Finds Love
The Lovely Liar

Autobiographical and Biographical:

The Isthmus Years 1919-1939
The Years of Opportunity 1939-1945
I Search for Rainbows 1945-1976
We Danced All Night 1919-1929
Ronald Cartland (With a foreword by Sir Winston Churchill)
Polly – My Wonderful Mother
I Seek the Miraculous

Historical:

Bewitching Women
The Outrageous Queen (The Story of Queen Christina of Sweden)
The Scandalous Life of King Carol
The Private Life of King Charles II
The Private Life of Elizabeth, Empress of Austria
Josephine, Empress of France
Diane de Poitiers
Metternich – The Passionate Diplomat

Sociology:

You in the Home
The Fascinating Forties
Marriage for Moderns
Be Vivid, Be Vital
Love, Life and Sex
Vitamins for Vitality
Husbands and Wives
Men are Wonderful
Etiquette
The Many Facets of Love
Sex and the Teenager
The Book of Charm
Living Together
The Youth Secret
The Magic of Honey
The Book of Beauty and Health
Keep Young and Beautiful by Barbara Cartland and Elinor Glyn
Etiquette for Love and Romance
Barbara Cartland's Book of Health

Cookery:

Barbara Cartland's Health Food Cookery Book
Food for Love
Magic of Honey Cookbook
Recipes for Lovers
The Romance of Food

Editor of:

'The Common Problem' by Ronald Cartland (with a preface by the Rt. Hon. the Earl of Selborne, P.C.)

Barbara Cartland's Library of Love

Library of Ancient Wisdom

'Written with Love' Passionate love letters selected by Barbara Cartland

Drama:

Blood Money
French Dressing

Philosophy:

Touch the Stars

Radio Operetta:

The Rose and the Violet (Music by Mark Lubbock) Performed in 1942

Radio Plays:

The Caged Bird: An episode in the life of Elizabeth Empress of Austria. Performed in 1957

General:

Barbara Cartland's Book of Useless Information with a Foreword by the Earl Mountbatten of Burma.
(In aid of the United World Colleges)

Love and Lovers (Picture Book)

The Light of Love (Prayer Book)

Barbara Cartland's Scrapbook
(In aid of the Royal Photographic Museum)

Romantic Royal Marriages

Barbara Cartland's Book of Celebrities

Getting Older, Growing Younger

Verse:

Lines on Life and Love

Music:

An Album of Love Songs sung with the Royal Philharmonic Orchestra.

Film:

The Flame is Love

Cartoons:

Barbara Cartland Romances (Book of Cartoons) has recently been published in the U.S.A., Great Britain, and other parts of the world.

Children:

A Children's Pop-Up Book: 'Princess to the Rescue'

Author's Note

WHEN IN 1928 I visited Egypt and saw the recently discovered Tomb of Tuten Khamun, I learned that balls of incense had been found in it.

From the earliest dynasties the Pharaohs used it as an offering to the gods of Egypt.

Incense was also used by the Babylonians for purification and to please their gods, and incense burners have been excavated from the Minoan graves in Crete.

The Greeks and Romans, especially the latter, burned it in vast quantities in their Temples. The spreading of the fragrance of the incense and the ascending smoke was a visible sign of the prayers and aspiration towards Heaven of the faithful worshipping their gods.

The trees from which the best frankincense and the shrubs from which myrrh was extracted grew only in Southern Arabia and a very substantial trade developed to meet the requirements of other countries. Huge camel caravans travelled 1,700 miles up the length of the Arabian Peninsula, along the great Incense Route, carrying their precious commodities.

Richard Burton was the most exciting phenomenon of his generation. He made considerable and significant contribution to the World in the field of Literature and Geography. He was also a Poet, Traveller, Soldier, Diplomat, Inventor, Explorer, Author, Archaeologist, Linguist, Anthropologist, an accredited student of Religions and undoubtedly of pornography.

Many biographies have been written about him but I have always felt when I look at his picture that they do not really do him justice. He was too big for the age he lived in, too mysterious and exciting.

Now he is dead, there is no way we can really understand the magic he radiated while he was alive. Perhaps he will be remembered most by those who read the 'Arabian Nights' and realise that he it was who first translated it.

On the marble plaque besides the Arab tent at Mortlake where Richard Burton is buried is inscribed Justin Huntly McCarthy's sonnet:

> Oh last and noblest of the Errant Knights
> 　The English Soldier and the Arab Sheikh
> Oh Singer of the East . . . . . .

Chapter One

1881

THE MARQUIS of Anglestone drove back to his house in Park Lane thinking surprisingly that he had enjoyed the luncheon.

Usually, when he was invited to No. 10 Downing Street with a Prime Minister, his heart sank.

There were of course exceptions like Benjamin Disraeli.

He unfortunately had lasted only six years, but the Marquis found on the whole that Prime Ministers were exceedingly boring.

He had not, therefore, looked forward to luncheon, his host being Mr. Gladstone.

However, he found to his relief that the rest of the party were extremely interesting.

They discussed mostly Foreign Affairs which interested him a great deal more than domestic ones.

He also took part in an animated discussion with the Secretary of State for India on conditions in the East.

Because the Russian Ambassador was present, they had to speak in lowered voices, and that somehow had made it all the more intriguing.

The Marquis was a very intelligent man, and, although few of his friends were aware of it, was keenly interested in matters pertaining to the Orient.

He had a secret hope that one day he would be invited by the Queen to be either Viceroy of India, or Governor of some part of her far-flung Empire.

He knew at the moment, however, that he was considered too young and, by the majority of Society, too frivolous.

What had really happened was that because he was so handsome, so wealthy and had so many enviable possessions, it was impossible for women to leave him alone.

What was more, if it was an *affaire de coeur*, regrettably to lose their hearts.

The Marquis had long ago decided he had no intention of marrying.

This however was something he did not discuss with other people.

His childhood had been clouded by knowing that his father and mother were positively miserable together.

They behaved, as was expected, with all possible decorum in public.

It was only those living in the house who were aware they had what amounted to a strong dislike of each other.

The Marquis had adored his mother, who was a very beautiful woman, and he had also admired and respected his father.

Therefore the fact that they were incompatible had left a scar which remained even now when he was nearly thirty-three.

When he thought about it, every instinct in his body shrank from the idea of living with a woman he did not love, merely for propriety's sake. He was sure she would feel the same about him.

This was unlikely as most women found him irresistible.

They flung themselves, inevitably, into his arms almost before he had asked their names.

At the same time, as he was honest, and also introspective, he admitted that his affairs did not last long.

It was he who was bored first.

It seemed to him extraordinary that a beautiful woman who would seem utterly desirable when he first met her should, on closer acquaintance, be what he could only describe as a 'crashing bore'.

He found himself fighting against being aware of exactly what she was going to say.

At not even having to guess at what she was thinking.

He tried to tell himself that a woman's role in life was to grace a man's table and, naturally, his bed.

He could sharpen his intelligence when he was with his men-friends.

But he had found out for himself that beauty was not enough!

He was therefore tired of finding, when he was not making love, that the most alluring woman really had nothing to say that was worth listening to.

"What is the matter with me?" he would sometimes ask himself.

Over the years he had found no answer to the question.

As he stepped out of his exceedingly smart carriage which he usually used only in the evenings, he realised that the air was crisp.

The sun still had some warmth in it and it was unusually mild for March.

"I will go riding," the Marquis decided.

He walked up the red carpet.

It had been hastily run down over the front steps as his horses turned in at the semi-circular drive in front of Anglestone House.

As he passed through the open front door, the Butler, an elderly man who had been with his father before he had inherited, moved forward to say:

"Lady Hester Wynn is waiting for Your Lordship in the Drawing-Room."

The Marquis frowned.

"Did you not tell Her Ladyship I was out?" he asked after a moment.

"I told Her Ladyship we were uncertain of what time Your Lordship'd be returning, but she insisted on waiting."

The Marquis handed his hat and gloves to a waiting footman.

Then he walked slowly up the curved staircase to the Drawing-Room which was on the First Floor.

It was a room perfectly designed for the reception of a large number of guests.

The Marquis was therefore aware of the reason why Lady Hester had not been shown into his Study.

It was far more intimate but his Butler as well as the rest of the staff was aware that she no longer played an important part in his life.

They had had a fiery and yet somewhat unsatisfactory affair the previous Autumn.

Lady Hester was exceedingly beautiful and had undoubtedly the most perfect figure of any woman in London.

The Marquis had found her, like all the others, a stimulus to a man's body, but not to his mind.

When the shooting season started at the end of October he had gone to the country.

On his return he had made no effort to renew his intimate acquaintance with Lady Hester.

Actually, it was one of his few affairs which had come to an abrupt end without tears and recriminations.

These continued with plaintive pleas, with scenes with which he was only too well acquainted.

He wondered now, as the footman hurried ahead to open the Drawing-Room door, what Hester wanted of him.

He remembered since Christmas she had been having a somewhat indiscreet affair with the Italian Ambassador.

Before there had been — for the moment he could not remember his name — a very good-looking man.

He sometimes met him at White's, his London Club.

The door opened and he walked into the Drawing-Room.

Lady Hester was standing at the window.

Having pulled aside a muslin curtain she was looking out into the garden.

In the summer it could look very attractive when the Marquis entertained.

There were trees on which could be hung Chinese lanterns, and paths that could be outlined with fairy-lights.

There were also several discreet little arbours where those who sat in them could not be seen.

It flashed through the Marquis's mind that Hester was remembering how he had kissed her in one of those arbours the very first night they met.

She had certainly not been reluctant.

He had known when his lips met hers that the fires of passion were already burning fiercely within her.

Later he was to find that they were insatiable.

Now he thought as he walked across the room, his feet making no sound on the Aubusson carpet, that Hester was looking very lovely.

A great number of men had eulogised over the perfection of her classical features.

They wrote poems to the sky blue of her eyes, and the spun gold of her hair.

She could look, the Marquis thought with a little twist of his lips, like a proud, untouched goddess who might just have descended from Olympus.

She would, however, become when he touched her, as vicious as Medusa.

He remembered she had been almost murderously jealous of him.

He had at one time been apprehensive in case she physically assaulted any other woman to whom he had momentarily paid attention.

The six months they had spent together had certainly been unforgettable.

Yet the Marquis knew that, beautiful though she was, he was relieved that Hester was no longer in his life.

She waited, and he knew it was deliberate, until he reached her before she turned from her contemplation of the garden.

"This is a surprise, Hester!" he said.

"I thought that is what you would think," she answered, "but I had to see you on an important matter."

"I do not wish to sound rude when I express the hope that it will not take long," the Marquis answered. "I am just about to go riding."

Hester laughed, a pretty if artificial sound.

"Horses! Always horses!" she exclaimed. "How can any woman hope to compete with a thoroughbred Arab mare?"

The Marquis did not deign to answer.

He merely walked to the fireplace to stand with his back to the mantelpiece waiting for Hester to join him.

She came towards him slowly.

He knew she was deliberately inviting him to admire the slimness of her waist, the manner in which her tight-fitting gown revealed the curves of her breasts.

Her long neck rose like a swan's above her three-row necklace of perfect pearls.

The Marquis however was looking not at her body, but at her face. He knew by the expression in Hester's eyes that she was up to mischief of some sort.

He invited her to sit down in one of the tapestry-covered gilt chairs.

Instead she stood directly in front of him, tipping back her head a little to look into his eyes.

It was a pose he had seen often before and he was well aware that most men would find it impossible not to kiss the curves of her cupid's-bow lips.

Their arms would automatically reach out to encircle the softness of her body.

Instead he said with a mocking note in his voice:

"Well, Hester, what is it?"

"Quite simply, Virgil," she answered, "and I hope you will be pleased at the news. I am going to have a baby!"

For a moment there was silence. Then the Marquis raised his eyebrows.

"I congratulate you!" he said. "And who is the lucky father?"

"Who but yourself!"

"That is impossible, as you well know!" the Marquis replied. "If this is your idea of a joke, Hester, it is not mine!"

"I am not joking, Virgil," she replied, "and I can imagine no better position for my child, especially if it is a boy, than to be able to call the Marquis of Anglestone his father!"

The Marquis looked at her and now his grey eyes were hard as steel.

"Are you attempting to blackmail me?" he enquired.

"An ugly word for a request for you to show yourself both generous and just."

"If you expect me to father another man's child, you are very much mistaken!" the Marquis said harshly.

"I am afraid you have little choice," Lady Hester replied.

Now she moved to sit down on the sofa.

The blue silk cushions made a perfect frame for her gown that was just a tone softer.

It was lightened by a small bunch of expensive orchids at the waist.

"I think you must make it clear to me exactly what you are trying to do," the Marquis said.

"I should have thought you could understand English," Lady Hester replied. "I am having a baby, and as the man in my life at the moment cannot provide for it, I suggest that we get married, and we shall be as happy as we were last Summer."

She spoke with a conviction which told the Marquis all too clearly that she was not joking, but meant every word she said.

Although it was incredible, he had the feeling that she really expected him to acquiesce to this appalling and quite ridiculous suggestion.

"If that is all you have to say, Hester," he said after a moment, "I think you are wasting both my time and yours. I am going riding."

Hester gave a little laugh.

"I expected, Virgil, you would fight like a tiger to prevent yourself from being taken to the altar, but this time the perennial bachelor has met his match!"

The Marquis did not reply, but merely started to walk towards the door. He had almost reached it when Hester said quietly:

"If you leave me, I shall go straight to the Queen!"

The Marquis stopped, but he did not turn round.

"I have already sent for my father to come South," Hester went on. "I am sure you would like him to be present at our wedding, and I want him to give me away."

Still the Marquis did not move, and she said in a deeper voice that had a touch of venom in it:

"On the other hand he will, I know, be prepared to go directly to Windsor Castle!"

The Marquis drew in his breath.

Slowly, with an inescapable dignity, he turned round.

"Why are you doing this?" he asked.

"I should have thought that was obvious," she retorted. "I have already told you that it's because there is no one else in my life at the moment who would be the right sort of father for my child!"

"You must be aware that no man in his right senses would accept such a preposterous idea."

"It is no use fighting against the inevitable," she answered. "I have always resented the way you pushed me off when you found somebody you thought was more attractive! I never could understand what you saw in that long-faced Mary Cowley!"

The Marquis did not miss the jealousy behind the words.

By now he had reached the fireplace.

He looked down at Hester sitting at her ease, and wondered what would happen if she put his hands around her long neck and throttled her.

He knew by the expression in her eyes that she was not as comfortable as she appeared to be, but her perfect lips were parted as she said:

"You are mine, Virgil, as you always have been, and now there is no escape."

The Marquis with an effort sat down in the chair next to hers.

"Now listen, Hester," he said, "you cannot imagine for one moment that I will agree to this nonsensical and insane idea of yours."

"I have told you, Virgil, that you cannot get out of it."

"That man you have talked about," the Marquis said, "I cannot remember his name. He is not married?"

"David Midway is as poor as a Church mouse," Hester replied, "and that is something I have no intention of being."

"Of course," the Marquis said quickly, "that can be partially remedied."

He was thinking quickly that if he gave Hester an allowance, even a large one, it would be preferable to her being his wife.

As if she was aware of what he was thinking she said quietly:

"I have always disliked the idea of being poor and besides, as you are aware, I shall grace the Anglestone diamonds."

"Dammit!" the Marquis swore, losing his temper. "I will not allow any woman to push me into the position of being married against my will, or fathering some other fool's bastard!"

"Strong words, Virgil!" Hester said, "I have never known you swear in front of a woman."

"You are not an ordinary woman, as you are well aware!" the Marquis snapped. "What you are trying to do is unprincipled and, in my opinion, criminal!"

"That was not something you thought when we were so happy together last Summer!" Hester pouted. "I can remember moments, Virgil, when you were quite poetical! Especially when you gave me a string of black pearls because they made my skin look so white."

The Marquis gave an exclamation of disgust and, rising, walked across to the window.

He remembered all too well how Hester had pleaded with him to give her the pearls which she had seen in Bond Street.

He had done so somewhat reluctantly, as they were very expensive.

She had then paraded herself in front of him wearing only the pearls with the desired effect and he had carried her to bed.

Now he asked himself how he could ever have become involved with her.

She had turned a pleasant 'affair' between two adult people into a nightmare of horror.

Lady Hester had when she was sixteen become involved with a very undesirable man, who was an employee of her father the Duke of Rothwyn.

The Duke had very quickly sent him packing and married his daughter off to the first suitor to be bowled over by her beauty.

Unfortunately, he was almost as old as the Duke.

Within two months of the marriage, Hester was behaving outrageously with a French *Comte*, whom she and her husband had met on their honeymoon.

He was the first of a long procession of lovers.

Then, after five years of marriage, Hester's husband died of a heart-attack.

Either his anger over her behaviour, or the excesses she expected from him had been too much for his constitution.

Hester was undoubtedly the most beautiful widow the Social World had ever seen and when she turned her blue eyes in the direction of the Marquis, he had found it impossible to resist her.

It was only now he realised fully what a fool he had been.

He should have known from the first moment of their acquaintance that Hester was not a normal woman in any sense of the word.

To be married to her, he knew, would be to exist in an indescribable hell.

And yet, for the moment, he could think of no possible

means of escape and the prison walls seemed to be closing in on him.

He knew Hester well enough to know that she was speaking without exaggeration when she said that she was prepared to go to the Queen.

He knew too, that the Duke would not hesitate to do what his daughter wanted.

The Duke's estate in Northumberland was run-down, the house was in a bad state of repair.

Its owner was faced with a pile of unpaid debts.

If the Duke was determined to have a rich and important son-in-law, then there was no man in the whole of the Social World better able to fill the bill.

"What can I do?" the Marquis wondered.

He felt as if his head was full of cotton-wool, and it was impossible to think.

"Well, then, Virgil?" Hester asked.

He knew she was reading his thoughts, and it infuriated him.

"Come back to me," she said, "and I will tell you what we are going to do."

"Let me make a suggestion," the Marquis parried.

He walked towards her as he spoke, and she knew by the squareness of his chin and the tightness of his lips how angry he was.

"I will give you £10,000 a year," he said, "until such time as you marry somebody so rich that you do not need it."

"£10,000 a year?" Hester repeated. "Do you really believe that would attract me when I can be your wife, the Marchioness of Anglestone?"

He made a furious exclamation but did not speak and she went on:

"I shall have thousands more than that at my disposal, besides enjoying my hereditary position at Court?"

It was with the greatest difficulty that the Marquis did not strike her.

His mother had been a Lady of the Bedchamber, as was traditional for all the Marchionesses of Anglestone.

He could not bear to think of Hester in his mother's

place, not only at Court but in the country, in his house at Newmarket and his Hunting Lodge in Leicestershire.

The idea made him want to murder her.

He knew only too well how appallingly she behaved and how his friends would pity him while being too afraid to say anything openly.

With a tremendous effort he forced himself to ask:

"What will you take?"

"A wedding-ring!" Lady Hester replied.

Now there was a look of malice in her eyes, and he knew she was enjoying her feeling of power over him.

She was burning him at the stake, and the more he screamed and cried in his agony, the better she would be pleased.

He hated her so violently that only years of self-control prevented him from shouting at her and knocking her down.

He was silent because he dared not allow himself to speak.

After a moment she said triumphantly:

"I have won, Virgil, and there is no way out! Now listen to what we are going to do."

She bent a little forward in her chair, raising her face as she did so, and he knew it was one of the poses she practised and which every man who watched her found alluring.

"When Papa arrives," Hester said, "we will let him into our happy secret, and then arrange a quiet wedding."

She thought the Marquis was about to speak and went on hastily:

"I am sure that is what you would prefer, and if we go away on our honeymoon as quickly as possible, no one will be surprised when the baby is born prematurely in seven months' time."

The Marquis's lips tightened and Hester continued:

"You may be angry now, but I think in the future you will realise that I would be a much more accommodating wife than some unfledged girl who would bore you within two weeks of your marriage."

The Marquis wanted to say that she bored him now, but thought it undignified.

"We shall be very happy together on the whole," Hester said, "but if later, when our child is born, you have 'other interests' I will not interfere, any more than I would expect you to interfere with mine."

She made a little gesture with her hands as she said:

"Nothing could be more civilised."

"There is nothing civilised about your behaviour!" the Marquis remarked, as if he could not help himself.

"That is what you always said you enjoyed about me," Hester parried. "You said I was . . as fast as the wind, as sharp as the frost, and soft as the snow!"

She gave a little laugh.

"Dear Virgil! Really very poetical!"

She got up to stand in front of him.

He could smell the exotic French perfume she used and recognised it.

He remembered washing it off his own skin.

It had remained like a ghost on the pillow long after she had left him.

"I will go now, Virgil," she said, "but do not forget to call on me tomorrow evening, when Papa should have arrived."

She made a little movement as if she would touch him, then with a flounce of her silk skirt turned away.

Only when she reached the door did she look back to say softly in a coaxing voice which he knew meant she wanted something:

"Dear Virgil, we shall be very happy, and I think you ought to give me a present to commemorate this wonderful moment when you promised to marry me!"

The Marquis clenched his fists, then, as the door shut behind Hester, he raised his arms towards the ceiling.

It was as if he beseeched the gods for help in the most terrifying situation he had ever encountered.

* * *

It was a quarter-of-an-hour later before the Marquis could bring himself to leave the Drawing-Room and walk down the stairs.

The Butler in the hall looked at him apprehensively as if expecting an order.

"My carriage!" the Marquis said sharply, and went into his Study.

It was a very attractive room with his writing-desk in the window and pictures of horses by Stubbs and Sartorious on the walls.

The newspapers were arranged on a stool in front of the fire.

He glanced at them and knew that in a day or so Hester would expect their marriage to be announced in '*The Times*' and '*The Morning Post*' and he felt himself shudder at the thought.

How could he accept such a woman as his wife?

How could he accept another man's child as his?

The questions seemed to be shouted at him from the very walls of the room.

Yet his brain could not tell him of any way out of the impasse in which he was caught like an animal in a trap.

He was not so foolish as to be unaware that the whole of the *Beau Monde* had talked about him and Hester last year.

When he had gone to the country to avoid her there was no particular reason that the gossips should think that their *affaire* had finished.

He had the idea, although he was not sure, that she had gone back to her father's home soon afterwards.

He thought, therefore, David Midway had spent some time in November with her in the country.

The Italian Ambassador had taken his place immediately after he had left, for he knew that she had started an affair with him this year.

But Hester would not be satisfied with one man for any length of time. Midway was good-looking, amusing, presentable and his father was a Baronet but he was also poor.

In a way the Marquis could understand the twisting manner in which Hester had worked out that he should be the father of her child.

At the same time he was sure she was intending to enjoy herself with anyone else who took her fancy.

The whole thing made him feel sick.

He had to face the fact however that if, as Hester had threatened, the Duke went to the Queen she would send for him.

Then there would be nothing he could do but obey her command and marry Hester.

The Queen was very strict about the slightest breath of scandal concerning those who occupied positions of importance at Court.

The Marquis's father had been Master of the Household for many years, and he knew it was only a question of time before he was offered the same position.

His mother had been a Lady of the Bedchamber. The Queen had always made it very clear how fond she was of her.

Because the Queen liked handsome men, the Marquis was aware she had often singled him out for small attentions which he had enjoyed.

This was partly because it had been amusing to see the envy it had caused amongst the Royal household.

If he defied the Queen and refused to do what she wished he would, to all intents and purposes, be exiled.

The Marquis did not delude himself into thinking that everybody loved him.

He was well aware that a great many of his contemporaries were envious of his prowess on the race-course.

They were also jealous because he attracted the beautiful women they coveted for themselves.

He had recently offended an influential Statesman by spiriting away from under his very nose an attractive little ballet dancer from Covent Garden.

The Marquis had installed her in a pleasant house in St. John's Wood. She had fallen in love with him, which actually broke all the rules.

She had therefore merely laughed at the discomfiture of the Statesman who had found her first.

The Marquis had laughed too.

Now he realised that the gentleman in question would be only too eager to take his revenge.

He would make things at Court even worse than he already anticipated they would be.

"What can I do? What the devil can I do?" he asked himself.

The Butler informed him that his carriage was at the door and he walked from his Study wondering where he could go.

He wanted to ask somebody's advice, but for the moment, he could think of no one in whom he could confide.

When he stepped into the carriage, the footman waited with the door open for his order. He said the first thing that came into his head:

"Take me to White's."

The door was shut, the footman clambered up on the box beside the coachman and they moved off.

As the Marquis glanced automatically at the front door he saw his Butler and two flunkeys bowing as he left.

He had a sudden terrifying feeling that Hester was already sitting beside him, and from now on he would never be rid of her!

It took him only ten minutes to reach St. James's.

The carriage drew up outside White's.

Telling his coachman to wait, the Marquis walked into his Club.

He was looking for a familiar face and a friend who could, by a miracle, find a solution to his problem.

It was with a sense of relief that he saw Lord Rupert Lidford sitting in the Morning Room, in conversation with two other men.

Lord Rupert looked up, saw the Marquis and exclaimed:

"Here is Anglestone! We will ask him what he thinks."

The two men murmured their agreement and the

Marquis sat down beside them. A Club Steward came forward to ask if he wanted anything to drink.

"A large brandy and soda!" he replied sharply.

He was aware as he spoke that Lord Rupert looked at him in surprise. The Marquis was well known for being abstemious.

Because he took part in many races, riding his own horses, he kept his weight down by eating sparingly and drinking very little.

Now he knew that never in his life had he wanted a strong drink more than he did at the moment.

"What we are talking about, Virgil," Lord Rupert said by way of explanation, "is Richard Burton."

The Marquis looked blank and one of the men said:

"You know who he is — the chap who has written a number of books and is bringing out another called '*The Kasidah*'."

"He is also the fellow who went to Mecca in disguise," another man chimed in.

"That was in 1853," Lord Rupert added, "and what we are saying is that no one today would be brave enough to face certain death merely out of curiosity."

"Do you really believe we are all chicken-hearted?" the third man, Lord Summerton asked.

"Of course we are!" Lord Rupert replied. "We have all grown soft, and while a great amount of the world remains unexplored, we are all too lazy to look at it."

"That is very scathing, and I do not believe it!" Lord Summerton argued.

"Can you see Virgil disguised as a dirty pilgrim?" Lord Rupert asked, "and risking his life to see the 'Forbidden City'?"

He laughed.

"I would bet a thousand pounds against it!"

"I will take you!" the Marquis declared.

There was a moment of stupefied silence. Then Lord Rupert said:

"Did you say you would take me?"

"I will go to Mecca," the Marquis went on, "and when I

return, entitled to wear the green turban, you shall pay me a thousand pounds!"

He stopped speaking as the servant returned and put a glass down beside him.

He took a long drink.

"You are insane!" Lord Rupert exclaimed.

* * *

Driving with the Marquis from White's to Park Lane, Lord Rupert asked:

"Are you serious, Virgil, or is this some extraordinary joke I do not understand?"

"I have never been more serious," the Marquis replied, "and I shall leave England tomorrow morning."

"Tomorrow!" Lord Rupert exclaimed.

"If I reach Mecca or not," the Marquis went on, "it is the answer to a question for which I have no solution — whether or not I should marry Hester Wynn!"

"Good God!" Lord Rupert exclaimed. "I thought that was over."

"It was," the Marquis replied. "But now she tells me she is having a baby."

Lord Rupert stared at the Marquis as if he could not believe his ears.

Then he said:

"Are you telling me the truth?"

"Hester has made it very clear that if I do not marry her, the Duke will speak to the Queen!"

"But — it is not your child!"

"No one knows that better then I do," the Marquis said, "I swear to you, Rupert, I have not touched her since last September!"

"If you ask me, I think it is Midway's!" Lord Rupert remarked.

"That is what I think," the Marquis agreed. "But he has no money, and Hester wishes to be a Marchioness!"

"She wishes to be your wife!" Lord Rupert contradicted. "Quite frankly, Virgil, when you finished with her I was rather surprised that she left as quietly as she did."

"So was I," the Marquis admitted, "but now she is seeking her revenge."

"And you think by running away . . ?" Lord Rupert began.

"I would fly to the moon, or dive down to the very depths of Hell if it would save me from marrying her!" the Marquis said violently.

I can understand you feeling like that," Lord Rupert said soothingly, "but – Mecca!"

"It was stupid of me not to think of it for myself," the Marquis said. "Then, when you spoke of it just now, I knew it was the answer to the question I have frantically been asking myself."

He paused before he said:

"But I need your help."

"You know I will do anything you ask of me."

"I have to go away without it being obvious or making it possible in my absence for Hester to go to the Queen."

Lord Rupert was listening.

He was a good-looking young man and had been at Eton with the Marquis where they had been great friends and they had gone up to Oxford together.

They had joined the same Regiment in which they had both served for five years before the Marquis inherited his title.

Because they wanted to be together, Lord Rupert had bought himself out of the Army. Now he spent more time with the Marquis than he spent in his own home.

They were more or less inseparable.

"What I want you to do," the Marquis said, as if he was thinking aloud, "is to make quite sure that our bet is talked about amongst our friends, while of course taking care it does not get into the newspapers."

"Go on!" Lord Rupert prompted as the Marquis paused.

"I am thinking it will be difficult for Hester to make a scene at my disappearance, when I am doing something which will be considered sporting, at least I hope so, among my contemporaries."

"They will think it is sporting," Lord Rupert said, "but personally, I think it is lunacy!"

"If Richard Burton can do it, so can I!" the Marquis exclaimed.

"It might not be so easy now the Moslems realise that he infiltrated their sacred and forbidden City."

"Do they know that?"

"He has written about it," Lord Rupert replied, "and I suppose some of them can read!"

"It is my only chance," the Marquis said desperately, "and I am very grateful to you, Rupert, for putting the idea into my head."

"That is certainly something I did not intend!" Lord Rupert replied. "I was just contradicting Summerton because he is always so pompous about everything!"

"I, too, find him a bore," the Marquis remarked.

Lord Rupert was silent for a moment. Then he said:

"You will take care of yourself, Virgil? According to Burton, and I have read some of the articles he wrote about Mecca, the punishment for violating the most sacred Moslem shrine is a very unpleasant and a slow and agonizing way of dying!"

"That would be better than having to marry Hester!"

"There I agree with you and I cannot imagine what you saw in her."

The Marquis did not reply.

He never talked about his love-affairs, not even to Lord Rupert, who was his closest friend.

He would in fact have preferred to go off into the blue without confiding in anybody that he had to do so. But he knew that he needed Rupert's help.

He trusted him as he would never have trusted anybody else.

When they got back to the house the Marquis sent for his secretary and started to give him authoritative orders.

Listening to him, Lord Rupert thought that perhaps in a way this was the best thing that could happen.

He had a deep affection for the Marquis and thought of him as the brother he had never had.

He had therefore been perturbed, for some time although he would not say so, at the manner in which the Marquis wasted his brain.

He had also wasted his exceptional qualities on women who were not worth it. Lord Rupert had disliked Lady Hester from the first moment he had met her.

He knew she was the type of woman who wished to ensnare every man who came within her orbit and he had watched with dismay the manner by which she made a dead set at the Marquis.

That she was beautiful was indisputable, but Lord Rupert was aware how relentless she was.

He knew that beneath the beauty of her appearance, she was avaricious, greedy and completely and absolutely selfish.

"It would certainly kill Virgil to be married to her!" he thought now.

Then when the Marquis joined him, they started to think of everything he would need on his voyage.

Also what precautions he should take to prevent himself from being discovered when he tried to enter Mecca.

Chapter Two

THE MARQUIS left London early in the morning with only Lord Rupert to see him off.

As they talked together for a few minutes in the Marquis's private railway carriage which had been attached to the train for Dover, Lord Rupert asked:

"When shall I see you again?"

He spoke in an almost despairing voice, feeling that his friend was going off on a wild adventure without really considering that it might cost him his life.

"I will be back as soon as it is possible," the Marquis replied.

"You mean," Lord Rupert said slowly, as if he was thinking it out for himself, "when Hester gives up the chase."

The Marquis's voice was hard as he answered:

"If it is true she is having a baby, then she will have to find herself a husband fairly quickly!"

Lord Rupert's eyes lit up as if he had not thought of that before: then he asked:

"How shall I get in touch with you?"

"That is a difficult question," the Marquis answered, "and I cannot help thinking that somewhere in Arabia will not be a very good address!"

Lord Rupert laughed.

"What will you do with the yacht?"

The Marquis considered it for a moment. Then he said:

"We know that submarine cables are now attached to every English port, and also I expect, Alexandria, Port Sudan and Aden. Any of those should find me, and I will inform my Captain to keep in touch."

"All I can say is that I hope to God you come back safely," Lord Rupert exclaimed.

"So do I, as it happens," the Marquis said, with a wry smile.

Because of the efficient way in which he ran his affairs, the Marquis's yacht – '*Sea Hawk*' – which was in Dover harbour, was ready to move out to sea almost as soon as he boarded her.

His Secretary had, as it happened, taken the precaution of sending a messenger on the midnight train to inform the captain of the Marquis's unexpected arrival.

The yacht was in consequence looking very spick and span with the seamen as smart as the brassware, and it was therefore impossible for the Marquis to find fault with anything on board.

He informed the Captain that they were heading for Alexandria.

Once they moved out of port, as the sky was overcast and the sea tempestuous, the Marquis did not have time to think about his own predicament.

During their passage through the Bay of Biscay there were occasions when the Marquis thought it was very unlikely that he would reach the Mediterranean let alone Mecca!

At Gibraltar there was a cable for him. When he opened it, he read:

"*YOUR PLAN GOING PERFECTLY. H. STUNNED BY THE NEWS. CLUB TALKING OF LITTLE ELSE BUT HAVE IMPRESSED SECRECY IMPORTANT FOR YOUR SAKE. MISSING YOU. RUPERT.*"

The Marquis smiled with satisfaction.

Then, thinking it unwise to keep the cable he tore it into pieces and made certain they were destroyed.

It was sunny in the Mediterranean, but the sea was not smooth and the Marquis was glad when he reached Alexandria.

As they steamed into the age-old port he found himself wishing he had somebody with him with whom he could talk about the history of Egypt.

He wanted a friend who was as interested in the Pyramids, the Pharaohs and the history of the Nile as he was.

He went ashore to stretch his legs.

He had to fight his way through the usual collection of beggars demanding *baksheesh* and gully-gully men producing miserable little day-old chicks from their pockets.

As he was returning to the harbour he saw a man whom he had not seen for many years.

"Good heavens, Anglestone!" Major John Anderson exclaimed. "You are the last person I expected to see in Egypt!"

"I cannot think why," the Marquis retorted.

Major Anderson laughed:

"I thought you were too busy dancing attendance on the Prince of Wales and escorting all the most beautiful women in London to patronise foreign shores."

"You are wrong and I am here!" the Marquis said.

"May I ask where you are going, and why?"

The Marquis had no intention of telling his friend the truth.

"As a matter of fact," he said, "I thought it would be interesting to see the Suez Canal, and perhaps to spend a little time in Cairo."

"That is where I have been," Major Anderson replied, "and if you do go to Cairo, have a word with Richard Burton. You will find him at Shepherd's Hotel."

The Marquis was instantly alert.

If there was one person he wanted to see at this particular moment, it was Richard Burton.

He had not read his *"Personal Narrative of A Pilgrimage to El Medinah and Meccah"* which had been published in 1855 but he had certainly heard a lot of people talk about it.

He thought, once he was at sea, that he had been very remiss in not bringing a whole collection of books with him.

He should read about the land he intended to visit, and certainly anything he could find about Mecca itself.

It suddenly seemed to him that the information which John Anderson had just given him was something which had been proclaimed.

It was almost as if the gods themselves were taking a hand in shaping his fate.

"You are quite certain if I go to Cairo that Burton will still be there?" he asked anxiously.

"I was with him three days ago," Major Anderson replied, "and I understood he had no intention of moving until he had obtained permission to explore for the gold he believes is to be found in abundance somewhere in Midian."

"Then I must go to see him," the Marquis said firmly.

He had not been listening to everything that Major Anderson had said.

All he wanted was his reassurance that Burton would still be there if he went to Cairo.

"Incidentally," Major Anderson added, "Burton is booked in as Dr. Abdullah — a Pathan."

Returning to '*The Sea Hawk*' the Marquis told his Valet to pack everything he required and two hours later was in a train proceeding to Cairo.

It was also allegedly a place where it was said if you waited long enough, everyone you knew would turn up there.

The Marquis arrived and, on finding that 'Dr. Abdullah' was in the Hotel, sent him a hastily written invitation to join him in his Suite.

While he was waiting for an answer, he thought over what he knew about him.

Burton was, the Marquis was well aware, one of the most unusual and certainly one of the most exciting men in the world.

He was an explorer who had visited many strange countries and written about each one of them.

Thinking back, the Marquis could remember people discussing Burton's book on "*Goa and the Blue Mountains*" and another called "*Falconry in the Valley of the Indus*".

He remembered reading fairly recently a book entitled "*Two Trips to Corilla Land*".

At the back of his mind he could also remember a Prime Minister, and he thought it was Gladstone, speaking very highly of Burton's experiences entitled "*The Rocky Mountains to California*".

Someone at the same luncheon, he could recall, had said that in his opinion, what Burton had written about the Nile Basin was a classic.

The Marquis could recall Richard Burton being talked of as a Soldier, an Inventor, an Archaeologist and an Anthropologist as well as a brilliant Linguist.

In fact, it had been a joke at White's when somebody had said that Burton could speak twenty-eight languages. A wit had added:

"One being Pornography!"

As he waited for a reply to his invitation, the Marquis found himself almost as excited as a schoolboy.

He was longing to meet a man who had risked his life, his health and had endured great hardship simply to travel through lands where no civilised man had ever been before.

The Marquis was intelligent enough to realise there were many great men, and that Burton was certainly one of them, to whom danger was a thrill.

It excited the mind and the spirit.

Although Burton must now be fifty-nine years of age, it did not surprise the Marquis that he wanted to search for gold in the Midian.

The door of his Sitting-Room opened and Burton came in.

The Marquis thought no man could look more overpowering and in a way exciting, just as he had expected.

Burton was wearing a burnous and his henna make-up.

But his strange, dark, hypnotic eyes, his high cheek bones, long drooping moustaches of which he was very proud, and his lean athletic form made him a fairytale figure.

There was something almost violently forceful about him and as they shook hands, the Marquis sensed the eagerness for life and adventure that vibrated from him.

He could hear his irrepressible joy of living in every word he spoke.

"I know about you, My Lord," Richard Burton said, "and I believe your horses are outstanding."

"I have certainly heard about you, Mr. Burton," the Marquis replied, "and I wish you every success with your new book which I understand is soon to be published."

"The '*Kasidah*' is being privately printed," Richard Burton replied, "and I hope when you read it you will think it is some of the best work I have ever done."

"I shall look forward to it eagerly," the Marquis smiled. "In the meantime, I would be extremely grateful for your help."

He indicated a chair and Richard Burton sat down and accepted a glass of champagne.

"How can I help you?" he asked.

"I want to emulate your example," the Marquis replied, "and enter Mecca!"

Richard Burton started and stared at the Marquis in astonishment.

"Is this a joke?" he asked.

"No, I am perfectly serious," the Marquis replied, "and I should be very proud to follow in your footsteps."

"But, my dear young man, it is impossible!" Richard Burton exclaimed.

"Why?" the Marquis enquired.

"Quite simply, because you would be discovered before

you could even set foot inside Mecca itself, let alone reach the Khaba!"

The Marquis's lips tightened and he said firmly:

"That is where I want to go!"

"Then I can only hope you have made your Will!"

The Marquis drank a little of his champagne before he said:

"It is too long a story to explain, but to extract myself from an uncomfortable situation, and because I have accepted a wager that I will visit Mecca, you can understand it will be impossible for me not to attempt to do so."

Richard Burton laughed and it was the deep laugh of a man genuinely amused.

"I understand, of course I understand," he said. "But I do not think you are driven by an inner need, as I am, to explore what has never been explored before, or to defy the gods themselves by pretending to be somebody you are not!"

"I do not believe," the Marquis said persuasively, "that without your help, I could succeed in entering Mecca."

"Have you considered how you would be able to manage without speaking any Arabic?" Richard Burton enquired.

The Marquis nodded.

"I realise that would be a stumbling-block," he agreed, "and I intend to find an Arab teacher. Incidentally, I am very quick at learning languages, knowing as I do the more traditional ones."

"Arabic is a little more difficult than most others," Richard Burton interposed.

"If I am still not proficient enough," the Marquis went on, as if Burton had not spoken, "I thought I could be escorted there by somebody I can trust, and pretend to be dumb. I might get away with it."

Again Richard Burton laughed.

"You might, and you might not," he said. "At the same time, I admire your spirit and your imagination. Let me think . . ."

He put his hand to his forehead as if to concentrate on the Marquis's problem. Then he said:

"I have a suggestion to make which I think you will find sensible. Forget Mecca for the moment, or rather, set it on one side and proceed first to South Arabia – in fact beyond Aden."

The Marquis was listening intently, and Richard Burton went on:

"Do not go near the English in Aden, but anchor in Qana, which is a Port about 300 kilometres East."

Richard Burton paused then continued:

"Qana was the original Port of the incense ships, and a Greek writer said that frankincense was known as 'the perfume of the gods'."

He smiled before he went on:

"It was certainly in demand by all civilised countries before Christ and was shipped from the Port of Qana."

The Marquis did not quite see how this affected him until Richard Burton continued:

"You will find in Qana a man who will help you with your guides, your camels and most important, your appearance."

The Marquis drew in his breath. This was exactly what he wanted.

"His name," Richard Burton went on, "is Salem Mahana and if you tell him I have sent you, he will do all he can to help you."

"I am very grateful."

"It will be a long pilgrimage from Qana to Mecca," Richard Burton warned, "but I feel you would be safer approaching the Holy City from the South, than the more usual route from the North."

His voice deepened as he said impressively:

"Whichever way you go, it will be extremely dangerous, and I suppose foolhardy. At the same time, if you succeed, it will give you something spiritual which you cannot achieve in any other way."

"That is what I would like to do," the Marquis said quietly, "apart from the wager."

"Then may Allah go with you," Richard Burton said, "and if you fail, I should warn you that the prolonged tortures they will inflict on you before you die, are beyond thinking about!"

The Marquis did not speak and Richard Burton rose to his feet.

"I have something in my room I want to give you," he said, and left.

The Marquis sat thinking of what Richard Burton had said.

He told himself he could not have been more fortunate.

He had the help of a man who was acknowledged as being one of the greatest explorers in the world.

He knew without being told that Burton thought it was very unlikely that he could enter Mecca and live.

The Marquis would not have been human if he had not asked himself whether taking such a risk was really justified.

Then he told himself that he had given his word and it was something he had to do.

To creep home now, admitting he was afraid would be worse than dying at the hands of fanatical Moslems.

"Dammit, I *will* do it!" he told himself fiercely.

At that moment Richard Burton came back into the room.

The Marquis could not guess what his gift would be.

It was certainly not the slim volume Burton held out to him.

"Is this one of yours?" he asked before Richard Burton could speak.

"No, it was written by a man whom I admire and who is a friend of mine — Professor Edmund Tewin."

The Marquis waited for Richard Burton to say more and he went on:

"You will perhaps be surprised when I tell you that it is about frankincense and myrrh, and describes the tremendous trade of which I have just spoken that took place in the past."

He paused to say more slowly:

"Where you are going is on the trail by which the caravans proceeded from Oman up through Arabia, passing close to Mecca."

The Marquis understood and Burton continued:

"When they reached Petra the incense was carried to Egypt, Rome and to Greece. A certain amount of it still arrives today in the same way that it did when the demand was enormous."

"You are suggesting," the Marquis said, "that I follow the trail as a trader."

Richard Burton nodded.

"It would be safer to do that and arrive in your own caravan. At the same time, Salem Mahana may have different ideas, and you must do as he tells you."

"I can only thank you from the bottom of my heart," the Marquis said, "for being so helpful."

"I can only hope that I am not mistaken in thinking this will be a safer way than any other," Richard Burton said. "But I would never discourage a man from exploring the world! Nothing is so satisfying as achieving something, when everybody expects you to fail."

The Marquis laughed.

"I can understand that, and I also hear that you have a new exploration in mind at this moment."

Richard Burton sat down and held out his empty glass.

"I am absolutely convinced," he said, "that gold is to be found in great abundance in Midian, a stretch of land twenty miles wide at Aquaba Weijh."

"Then I most certainly drink to your success," the Marquis remarked.

"And I to yours!" Richard Burton said, "And the fate of us both is in the hands of Allah!"

He raised his glass as he spoke.

* * *

Riding towards the Coast, Medina felt just a faint breeze from the sea against her skin.

It had been almost unbearably hot for the last ten miles.

Although she was riding a fast-trotting dromedary, she felt she would never reach Qana before it was dark.

She had known she would have been wiser to go slower.

She should have kept with the caravan of camels and the hand-picked Arabs who had served her father.

But she wanted to escape from the memories of the grace she had left in the hills above Maris.

She wanted to tell Salem Mahana what had happened before she faced her future alone.

It was therefore with a sense of almost inexplicable relief that she saw the black volcanic promontory which the Arabs called Hisn Al Ghurab (fortress of the ravens).

Now she had only a mile or so more to go.

The dromedary trotted with what to the Arabs was incredible swiftness over the sand.

Medina was this evening not thinking as she usually did of Qana in the days when it was the famous Port for the incense trade of Arabia.

Her father had told her that, at its peak in the 2nd century A.D. it had been estimated that South Arabia had sent more than 3,000 tons of frankincense every year to Greece and Rome.

A few thousand years earlier the Egyptians were using the 'perfume of the gods' as they called it, for Temple rites.

Medina could remember her father telling her that Herodotus, the Greek father of History, wrote in B.C. 450:

"The whole country is scented with Arabia's aromatics and it exhales an odour marvellously sweet."

As dusk fell and Medina reached Qana it was now very different from what it had been.

During the Middle Ages a sleepy town further up the coast had replaced Qana as the chief Port of Hadramant.

Now there were very few creaking wooden ships to be found there, or sacks and goat-skins filled with incense.

There were no half-naked longshoremen sweating and cursing.

No shouting soldiers, scribes, and money-changers, their noise sometimes lost in the bellowing of the camels.

Instead Qana was just a quiet, unimportant little town, except for one man.

Nobody took any notice as Medina rode through the scattered houses.

She passed a Mosque, on to where there was a rather better-looking house surrounded by a courtyard.

She rode into it.

An Arab boy who lay half-asleep on some steps rose slowly as she drew her dromedary to a standstill.

She made the animal kneel down, stepped on the ground and walked quickly up the steps in through the door which was standing ajar.

Inside there was a dark passage with which she was familiar.

She found her way to the end of it, and knocked on a door, and without waiting for an answer she opened it.

As she expected, sitting in a strange room ornamented with a surprising amount of what appeared at first glance to be clothes, weapons and ancient pots was Salem Mahana.

He was a large fat man, dressed in a long white robe and wearing a heavily jewelled *jambiyyn*, the traditional curved dagger of the Arab.

He was smoking his *hookah* but laid it aside as Medina appeared and gave an exclamation of delight.

"You are back!"

Medina made him an obeisance, then walking towards him sat down cross-legged at his side.

She was wearing a burnous and under it a *snab*.

This was a long shirt which reached from her neck to her ankles, fastening down the front.

On her head was a red *mahranah* — a silk head-cloth held in place by the *ukal* or fillets of knotted silk.

Her *hizam* or waist belt held a dagger.

It would have been impossible for any stranger to realise she was a girl.

Then as she glanced over her shoulder to see that the door behind her was shut, she pulled off her head-cloth and shook her head as if to release the tension of the ride home.

Her hair, which had been lying flat, seemed to spring to life.

It was cut short and fell in soft waves on either side of her small, fine-featured face. The sockets of her large eyes were outlined with *kohl* as were her eyebrows.

Now with her skin darkened with the same dye, to the coffee-colour of any Arab, she looked more like a woman.

So that it was not surprising that the men of the caravan, and indeed anyone in Qana with the exception of Salem Mahana, believed her to be a boy.

She did not speak, and intuitively Salem knew that something was wrong.

"Your father?" he asked.

Medina drew in her breath.

"Papa . . died at . . Marib."

"May Allah give him rest," Salem said automatically, "what happened?"

"He knew before we went that his heart was giving him trouble," Medina answered, "but as you know, he was so keen to go. Although I begged him to wait a little and to rest, he would not listen."

"Your father was an impatient man," Salem murmured.

"I have never known him in such good spirits," Medina went on, "then six days ago, when we went out alone at night to look for what he was seeking . . he started to dig and suddenly . . without any warning . . collapsed."

She paused and her voice was very moving as she said:

"I knew the moment I touched him . . that he was . . dead. I knew too . . it was the way he would . . have wanted . . to die."

"That is true," Salem said. "I am sorry! I will miss him. He was a great man."

"I . . I loved him," Medina said simply, "and I . . cannot face the future . . without him."

There was a childlike note in her voice and now she was no longer the young man who had come striding into the room, she was a woman, or rather, a girl, crushed by grief.

Her large eyes filled with tears.

"Oh, Salem, how can I . . go on without him?" she asked, and it was a cry that came from her heart.

"You will have to go home, my child," Salem said gently.

"I know," Medina answered, "but you have no idea how . . difficult that . . will be."

"You have relatives and friends in England?"

"Friends, no, relatives, yes, and they are not friendly either!" Medina replied.

She made a sound that was half a sob before she said:

"How can I . . face it? They were so angry with Papa because he took me with him. If I go back they will only tell me how . . wrong he was, and how can I listen to anyone . . abusing him when he was . . so wonderful?"

Salem did not reply.

He was puffing once again on his *hookah* and the water gurgling in it was the only sound in the room.

Medina looked around her a little wildly.

"I will not go home!" she said. "I will stay here, I will work for you! Heaven knows, you have enough disguises so that . . no one need ever know that I am . . most unfortunately . . a woman."

"You may think it unfortunate," Salem said quietly, "but your father often said to me that you were a very beautiful young woman, and it is time you married."

"I shall never marry!" Medina said firmly.

"Why not?"

"Because I have no wish to be a dull, conforming wife,

agreeing with everything my husband says, and finding life in England incredibly boring!"

She made a sound that was almost a cry as she held up her arms to say:

"Here with Papa, there has been so much to see, to talk about, to think over and to explore, not only in Qana but in my mind and . . of course in . . my heart."

She drew a deep breath.

"Oh, Salem, Salem! How could I . . bear it? How can I go home alone . . without Papa?"

Tears ran from her eyes down her cheeks and she wiped them away like a child with the back of her hand.

"You must put your trust in Allah," Salem said quietly, "but I also have a suggestion to make."

As if she knew what it would be Medina merely bowed her head.

Once again she wiped the tears from her eyes.

She felt a little ashamed of herself for being so demonstrative in front of Salem, but he was, however, the only friend she had in the world; the only person with whom she could be herself now that her father was dead.

It was ten years ago, when she was a child of eight, that Professor Edmund Tewin had walked out of his house in England. He left immediately after his wife's Funeral.

His relations and those of his wife had joined together.

They had explained to him that it was quite impossible for him to take his only daughter Medina with him on his travels.

His wife had gone everywhere with him in the nine years they had been married.

It had horrified her father and mother, her three sisters and two brothers. They had all disapproved of Edmund Tewin from the moment he had married Elizabeth.

That she had been supremely happy travelling the world what they had called 'like a gypsy' had not counted.

A member of a distinguished County family, her father had arranged for his daughter to marry the son of the Lord Lieutenant.

A young man, he had been swept off his feet by her beauty from the moment he had met her.

Elizabeth might have accepted him, had it not been that by chance she met Edmund Tewin.

He was the hero of her dreams, the type of man whom she had believed existed only in her imagination.

Edmund Tewin, then over thirty, had already gained fame by writing of his travels in Arabia.

He had decided never to marry as he had no intention of 'settling down' to be a country gentleman on the small allowance from his father and the money he was making from his books.

But, just as Elizabeth had known that he was the man who was the other half of herself, he had felt the same about her.

They were married within three weeks of their first meeting and left immediately for a honeymoon in Arabia.

It was still a country that was comparatively unknown.

The majority of the tribes who inhabited it were hostile to strangers.

It would have been a terrifying experience for most well-brought-up young women.

Elizabeth had loved it.

She would rather have lived on the razor-edge of danger with Edmund than sit on the throne of England!

The hardships they both endured and the books which Edmund wrote of their extraordinary experiences made them more in love every day they were together.

It was only after Medina was born that Edmund consented to have a home.

Elizabeth's father gave him a house on his estate.

They returned for Edmund to write his books after they had journeyed thousands of miles for the copy he required.

Then, when they came home after exploring the Sudan, Elizabeth was struck down with a strange Eastern disease. No English doctor could find a cure for it, or even diagnose it.

She had simply wasted away day by day.

She grew thinner until there seemed nothing left except her eyes still filled with love for her husband and her lips which told him how much she loved him.

She died after what had really been a very short illness.

Desperate with grief, Edmund found the house in which they had been so happy was a prison. He knew he had to escape as quickly as he could.

This was actually more or less what Elizabeth's family as well as his had expected.

What they had not anticipated, however, was that he intended to take Medina with him and there was a furious outcry to which he would not listen.

There was nothing they could do to stop him for a father was the Guardian of his own child and could therefore do what he wished.

He left England three days after Elizabeth was buried, taking Medina with him.

She had been called Medina because he had told Elizabeth that of all the Cities he had visited, Medina had been the most exciting and the most beautiful.

He never knew exactly why.

Yet it had always stuck in his mind that *Madinat al Nabi* – "The City of the Prophets" – had more to give those who visited it than any other City in the world.

Perhaps every explorer has a sacred shrine – the one place where his soul is raised into the sky, and he touches the stars that have always seemed out of reach.

That was what Medina had meant to Edmund Tewin.

His daughter was therefore christened Medina which, needless to say, the English found an outlandish and un-Christian name.

From the moment she travelled with her father, Medina was supremely happy.

To her, he was the most exciting, the most delightful and the kindest man in the whole world.

He taught her everything he knew himself, especially the Arabic of the different tribes.

She could claim to be from any part of Arabia and no one listening to her would suspect anything different.

She found it easier to travel with her father as a boy rather than a woman. As it would have been intolerable for her to have to cover her face, she cut her hair short.

She wore the clothes first of an ordinary Arab boy, then as she grew older, a young man,

She was fortunately tall enough to be about the right size.

From exercise and the frugal life they led when they were exploring, her body was thin and slender.

It was only Salem who knew the truth because he had been her father's friend for a long time.

He had helped Medina disguise herself with an enthusiasm which told her he appreciated that she was clever enough to get away with it.

Now, as he saw her crying, he realised how empty and hopeless her life would be without her father, and he said quietly:

"If I was doing what I know is right, I should insist on you returning to England. But I have, shall we call it, a treat that you will enjoy before you do so."

"What . . is that?" Medina asked.

Salem took a long draw on his *hookah* before he replied:

"Today a great English Lord came here to see me, sent by Mr. Burton."

Medina raised her head and now her body was no longer sagging with misery and despair and her eyes that were fixed on Salem bore a glimmer of hope in their depths.

She was not aware of it, but she was very lovely with her straight little nose and her heavily *kohled* eyelids.

There was a firmness about her chin and the way her head was poised with her long neck which any connoisseur of beauty would have appreciated.

When she wore her Arab head-dress it was difficult to see anything but its flapping sides. Because it came low down on her forehead it almost disguised her face.

"What did he want?" she asked as Salem paused.

"He wants to go to Mecca," Salem replied. "He told me

the truth because Richard Burton had said I would not help him if he was not honest with me."

"So he trusted you? That was wise?"

"He is a clever man! He sized me up," Salem replied, "I saw him doing it, and I knew in my mind exactly what he was thinking."

Medina was not surprised at this.

She knew that Salem had an extraordinary perception which made him aware of what people were thinking and feeling.

It ensured that, with the many people who came to see him from all over Arabia, he had never been deceived, nor was his confidence in them abused.

"Why should he want to go to Mecca?" Medina enquired.

"Again he was honest," Salem said, "and told me it was a wager, but it is much more than that!"

He paused, then wrinkled his forehead for a moment before he said:

"I knew without him telling me so that he is hiding from somebody — a woman, I suspect! To avoid her he had come to Arabia and decided to undertake this pilgrimage of which most men are afraid."

"Not surprisingly!" Medina said. "You will remember that man two years ago, who died in the most obscene manner!"

There was a note of horror in her voice which did not surprise Salem.

The camel-drivers had told of what had happened to the man who had chartered them and had been discovered attempting to enter the sacred Khaba.

The details of his torture and death had been enough to make the hardiest person feel sick.

He knew that Medina had been shocked into silence at the time.

It was unlikely she would forget what she had heard, and she said now:

"Surely you tried to dissuade him?"

"I have left that to you."

"To . . me?"

"Richard Burton told him I would find him a guide whom he could trust implicitly."

"You are telling . . me to guide . . him to Mecca?"

"It is a long way to Mecca," Salem said with a smile, "and there are many things for him to see on the way!"

Medina gave a little laugh and it took away the darkness of her eyes.

"Oh, Salem!" she said. "You are so crafty! Of course that is the right way to treat him. If you had tried to dissuade him he might have tried to reach Mecca without your help."

"As it is, *you* will help him," he said waving his hand in a gesture that was more explicit than words.

"But, of course!" Medina said, "And there are so many, many things to see on the way."

She thought for a moment before she said:

"I would like to meet this English Lord . . but first I must sleep."

"A room is waiting for you, my child."

Medina got to her feet as if she was suddenly very weary.

"Food will be brought to you," Salem went on, "and when you shut your eyes, remember your father is with Allah and at rest."

"I know Papa would . . want you to . . help me . . and that is what . . you have done . . already," Medina said in a soft voice.

She made Salem a little obeisance and taking up her head-dress, she put it on her head, pulling it down low over her forehead.

She went from the room.

Salem sat back against the cushions behind him.

"Allah go with her!" he murmured beneath his breath.

Chapter Three

WHEN THE Marquis left Richard Burton at Shepherd's Hotel, he went first to the largest bookshop in Cairo.

He bought every book they had on Arabia.

There were not many of them and they were mostly in French or German, which fortunately he could read.

There was one in English about the Arabs as a race which he thought he would find helpful.

He then went to the British Embassy and after some polite conversation he informed them that he needed an Arab teacher who could accompany him on a cruise down the Red Sea.

"I may stop for a while at Port Sudan," he said loftily, "but it rather depends how interesting I find that part of the coast."

The Ambassador's Secretary said he would see what he would do, and returned with an expression of triumph.

"We have a man on our staff, My Lord," he said to the Marquis, "who comes from Oman. He is intending to return home on his retirement, which will be in a month's time."

The Marquis's eyes lit up. He thought that once again fate was on his side.

"He is a well-known Scholar," the Secretary went on, "and if we release him a month before his retirement he would, I know, appreciate travelling as far as possible in the comfort of Your Lordship's yacht."

The Marquis could hardly believe his good fortune.

When he met the man, he knew immediately from the way he spoke that he was both erudite and civilised.

He had to wait for twenty-four hours while the Arab packed.

He sent a cable to Richard Burton to say if he wished to get in touch with him to cable the Consulate at Aden.

He knew there would be nowhere else in Southern Arabia where cables would be accepted.

He actually quite enjoyed his dinner with the Ambassador and he learnt a number of things about Arabia he had not known before.

The next day he returned to Cairo with his Arab teacher.

As soon as they were aboard he settled down to apply himself to learning Arabic with a concentration that would have surprised his London friends.

It was not as difficult as he had expected.

At the same time, he realised that to be proficient would take very much longer than the time he set aside for his lessons.

This was while he steamed through the Suez Canal which had been opened nine years earlier, and down the Red Sea.

By the time they had reached Jiddah which he was told was the port nearest to Mecca, he was glad he had taken Burton's advice to go further on.

The heat alone would have made him find the trek of 130 miles from the sea to the Sacred City extremely exhausting.

He was wise enough not to show his teacher that he was particularly interested in Mecca.

He concentrated on learning not only the language, but the customs of the different races about which Abdul Raie was unusually knowledgeable.

He was quite content to journey as far as Qana with the Marquis.

Then he intended to take a ship which would carry him on to Muscat which was his final destination.

Alternatively he might join a caravan making its way back to the harvesting areas of frankincense in the Dhofar region.

The Marquis was absorbingly interested in the book which Richard Burton had given him and he therefore searched the other books he had for more information about the incense trade.

It was something he had not known about in the past.

He found it fascinating to learn that, in the Roman world, incense was used in cremation rites.

He read that Nero had lavished the equivalent of a year's Arabian production on the funeral of his consort Poppaea.

Yet at the back of his mind was a stern determination to reach Mecca and that was more important than anything else.

He thought it would be not only the answer to Hester's claims on him, but it would also improve his image in his own eyes.

When they were moving through the Mediterranean the Marquis had taken a close look at himself, perhaps for the first time for many years, and he had not been impressed by what he found.

He realised, as Lord Rupert had, that he had been wasting his time on women who undoubtedly inflame a man's passions, but did nothing for his mind.

Hester, with her overwhelming beauty was, he thought, typical of a great number of other lovely creatures.

He had spent a great deal of his time with them, not to mention an inordinate amount of money.

He felt humiliated as well as furious at Hester's intention to foist the bastard son of another man onto him.

Yet he was honest enough to admit that it was something he might have anticipated.

The fault therefore lay not only with Hester, but also with himself.

"How can I have been so naive," he asked himself angrily, "as to have trusted her to behave decently when our affair was over?"

It was the same question he had asked as the '*Sea Hawk*' had pitched and tossed in the violence of the sea in the Bay of Biscay.

He had felt his fury rising like the green waves breaking over the bow of the ship.

Then he told himself sensibly that Hester was not worth his anger and he was to blame.

He knew the answer really lay in the fact that by now he should have married and settled down with a family, taking his place not only at Court, but in the County as his father had done before him.

He knew, however, that the young girls who his family would have considered admirable candidates for the position of Marchioness of Anglestone would have bored him to distraction.

The Marquis knew that, in aristocratic families, money was always spent on the oldest son who would inherit the title and the estate.

Other sons were fortunate in that they were sent to a Public School, then on to a University.

But the girls, being considered of little consequence, were educated by a Governess who knew little more than they did themselves.

The result eventually might be a beautiful, well-dressed and extremely elegant woman.

The Marquis was, however, aware that her brain would either be non-existent or undeveloped.

Her conversation would consist merely of the social gossip which took place in every *Boudoir*.

"How could I bear it?" he asked.

The answer was obvious and he told himself firmly, as he had done so often before, that he would never marry.

All the same, it was impossible to live without the fascination and allurement of women and the Marquis had succumbed easily to the blandishments of the sophisticated Beauties who abounded in the Social World.

That they were married or widowed made them very different from unfledged, shy and usually gauche virgins whom he met, and ignored wherever it was possible.

Hester had opened his eyes to the dangers to be encountered when consorting with a widow.

He had been careful in the past not to arouse the jealousy of a husband.

This would mean the gentleman insulted would call him out in a duel, now forbidden by the Queen.

Yet a duel would be better than to be blackmailed by Hester.

"Damn women! Damn all women!" the Marquis had said as the '*Sea Hawk*' carried him down the Mediterranean.

Now in the heat of the Red Sea, which he found overwhelming, he was saying the same thing.

Then in the book which Richard Burton had given him he found a spiritual stimulation that he had not expected.

He read of the magical properties of incense which Moses had believed would bring down the vengeance of God.

How originally incense was prescribed by the Ancient Egyptians in the '*Book of the Dead*' to ensure the safety of the departed in the after life.

He found himself entering a world he had never known and which awoke an interest and an excitement which was different and completely absorbing.

He could understand as he read on why Richard Burton had given him this particular book.

Although there was much useful material in the other books he had acquired, he kept returning to the "Perfume of the Gods".

He could never remember actually knowing that the incense that he had noticed in Catholic Churches was frankincense and had the feeling that when he smelt it again it would mean something different.

By the time the '*Sea Hawk*' sailed into the forgotten Port of Qana, the Marquis could speak Arabic fairly fluently and understand a great deal of what his teacher said.

He rewarded the man generously, then stepped ashore to find Richard Burton's friend.

He was conscious as he did so of a stirring of excitement.

It was rather like what he felt when he was on the verge of winning what had been an arduous race.

As he walked down the narrow street which led to Salem Mahana's house, he was unaware as he did so that the few people watching him were finding it hard to believe he had not come from another Planet.

Visitors to Qana, unless they were Arabs, were few and far between.

Those who did come were of little interest to the small traders and heavily veiled women who wandered from stall to stall in the market.

When Salem Mahana promised the Marquis that he would find him the right guide to take him to Mecca, the Marquis returned to his yacht.

He felt triumphantly that he had overcome the first obstacle on his pilgrimage to the Sacred City.

Everything so far had gone better than he expected and he could only pray that he would not be disappointed when he called on Mahana next day.

He was well aware that nothing was ever done in a hurry in the East, and he might have to stay in Qana for a week, perhaps more, before he could be on his way.

Yet he realised Salem Mahana was an exceptional man. He was certainly not somebody to whom he could give orders and expect them to be carried out 'at the double'.

The Marquis knew too that he had an authority which

he must respect if he was not to be sent away empty-handed.

He was perceptive enough to realise that it was not just a question of money.

There was something about Salem Mahana which was different from the Arabs he had met and talked to previously and also different from a large number of other men, in England or elsewhere.

The Marquis had the idea that the people who came to Mahana for help and the arrangements he could make were a personal interest.

It was as if he was an artist, a carpet-weaver, or perhaps a writer like Richard Burton.

What he was using was his craft, and his craft meant disguising Burton or himself, it was all part of a plan which the Marquis was sure Salem Mahana believed was directed by Allah Himself.

He was therefore quite prepared to leave himself completely in Mahana's hands and accept whatever he suggested.

He had been aware that, while he was sizing Salem Mahana up and using his perception as he did so, Mahana was doing exactly the same thing to him.

It was, he thought later that night when he was in his cabin, part of the inner knowledge of the East.

Here a man judged a man on what he felt instead of what he read about him on a piece of paper.

When the Marquis returned to Mahana's house the following day, he felt as if there were already new horizons for his mind.

Also something — he was not sure what — within himself was opening out like a 'lotus flower'.

Salem Mahana welcomed him in the same way as he had the day before.

They seated themselves in the strange room against the silk cushions on a carpet of exquisite Persian design, then tea was brought in handle-less cups by an Arab boy.

When he withdrew the Marquis found it impossible to contain his curiosity any longer.

"You have found me a guide?" he asked.

"I have found you, My Lord, the best and most experienced guide in the whole of Arabia!"

The Marquis nodded his appreciation of what he knew must be the usual Eastern exaggeration.

"He is young," Salem Mahana continued, "but Allah has given him the brain of a man much older than himself."

The Marquis raised his eyebrows at this and Salem continued:

"Ali is the son of a Sheikh, and he will therefore open doors that to ordinary travellers remain closed. You can trust him implicitly and your life is in his hands!"

"I understand," the Marquis said, "and I am very grateful. When may I meet this young man?"

"Ali Murad is here now. I will send for him."

Salem clapped his hands and a curtain covering one entrance to the room moved a little to show there was somebody behind it.

Salem gave a sharp order and the curtain was still.

"Do you think that I really have a chance of reaching Mecca?" the Marquis asked.

He wondered as he spoke if Salem Mahana would tell him, as Richard Burton had done, that it was impossible.

But the Arab merely replied:

"*Khayr Inshallah.*"

The Marquis knew that meant:

"It is well if Allah pleases."

It was the typical evasive Eastern reply which he might have expected.

There was just a faint twist to his lips as the curtain was pulled aside and Medina came into the room

It would have been difficult even for her father to have recognised her, dressed in the clothes of an Arab young boy of importance.

Salem Mahana had given her an *Abi* — a white cloak as worn by Sheikhs and Princes.

Under it Medina wore a silk shirt and a light pink coat with a plaid sash, into which she had thrust the traditional dagger which was ornamented with precious stones.

To complete it she wore pantaloons with tasteful edgings about the ankles and her lemon-coloured slippers were the most fashionable Constantinople cut.

In one hand she held a mother-of-pearl rosary, in the other a pipe with a jasmine stick and an amber mouth-piece.

She had laughed when she looked at herself in the mirror, but she realised that Salem had been wise when he had said:

"You must start off in the right way in being the equal of His Lordship and not just his paid servant."

She had added a white turban which had a length of soft silk to cover her chin and over the heavily kohled rims of her eyes she wore a pair of ugly steel spectacles.

She certainly looked unmistakeably masculine.

She walked into the room with an air of authority which she had seen so often amongst the Arab Sheikhs who were the autocratic rulers of their tribes.

Salem Mahana made a low obeisance to which Medina responded in a somewhat lofty fashion.

She bowed to the Marquis who had not risen at her entrance, but did so now as he held out his hand.

"This is Ali Murad, My Lord," Salem Mahana said unnecessarily, "and you will both look very different when you set out with your caravan."

"You have one arranged?" the Marquis asked.

"Your guide Ali will do that for you," Salem replied. "He knows the drivers who can be trusted and where the best camels are."

He paused to say quietly:

"They must not know who you are and, this afternoon, your yacht must leave Qana and proceed down the coast."

The Marquis did not reply, but he was listening:

"There is an inlet about two miles from here where you can disembark," Salem went on, "then you will return to stay here in my house."

"I see!" the Marquis said, "So the camel-drivers must not guess I am a foreigner!"

"It would be disastrous for them to do so," Salem replied.

"Then who am I?" the Marquis enquired with a smile.

"You are a friend of Ali — a trader in frankincense and myrrh, and you have a buyer who is waiting for you in Medina."

The Marquis's eyes sparkled. Now he understood what Salem was planning.

"All you have to do," the Arab went on, "is to leave everything in Ali's capable hands. Of course you will travel by the route which has been used for hundreds of years and which is known to us as the 'Frankincense Trail'."

"There are many things to see on the way," Medina said.

It was the first time she had spoken.

She had made her voice a little deeper, in keeping with her appearance which was not difficult for, although she had slept the sleep of exhaustion the previous night, she was still tired.

"What I want you to do now, Ali," Salem was saying, "is to go with His Lordship back to the yacht, taking with you only Nur."

"Who is Nur?" the Marquis enquired.

"He is Ali's special servant whom you will trust with your secret because he will dress you, disguise you, and look after you during the journey."

"I understand," the Marquis said.

"No-one else, and this is important, My Lord, must realise you are anything but an Arab."

"It is fortunate," Medina said quietly, "that his hair is dark. His skin will absorb henna, and after a few days in the sun it is doubtful if he will need it."

Salem laughed.

"That is true. He must look like an Arab and speak like an Arab — or else say nothing."

"I have learnt some Arabic," the Marquis said in that language, "but I realise I have a great deal more to learn."

Medina gave an exclamation of delight.

It was far better than she expected.

She realised, because Salem had told her, that the Marquis had learnt what he knew on his way from Cairo and that he was obviously intelligent.

She had, in fact, been astounded by the Marquis's looks when she had come into the room.

She had expected him to be distinguished-looking and she thought, too, he would have an air of authority, as most Englishmen had.

What she had not expected was to find him without exception the most handsome man she had ever seen.

Her father had spoken disparagingly of his English relations and those of her mother.

It had appeared they were all narrow-minded, critical and insular, so she had not expected the Marquis to be any different.

She was surprised to sense an eagerness and a vitality about him which was completely different from what she had expected, which was a rich man who was bored with life and was merely trying to find a new experience.

She had the feeling and she was sure she was not wrong, that the Marquis was not only interested in reaching Mecca so that he could boast about it.

She was sure that the most important spiritual City in the Arab world would mean something different to him.

Without any explanation she sat down cross-legged on a cushion beside the Marquis as a test to see if he could understand, and asked:

"What are you seeking?"

There were a dozen answers he might have given, but almost as her father would have done, he replied quietly:

"Enlightenment!"

For a moment Medina was so surprised that she could only stare at him through her spectacles.

Then it flashed through her mind that perhaps that was something Salem had told him to say.

She knew however, that he was speaking honestly and he was neither pretending nor in any way seeking her approval.

"What you will find," she answered, "may not be what you expect."

"I have not yet decided what I do expect," the Marquis replied, "but I want to learn and I am a willing pupil at your feet!"

He spoke in a language which she knew would be understood by anyone in the East and because he was speaking in Arabic it did not sound as strange as it would have done in English.

Salem clasped his hands together.

"That is good, very good!" he approved. "You learn fast, My Lord!"

"I had a good teacher," the Marquis replied, "but now he has left me, and I hope now that this young man will continue with my lessons so that by the time I reach Mecca I shall be word-perfect!"

"It rests in the hands of Allah," Salem murmured.

They talked for a little while longer, then Ali and the Marquis walked by a less-frequented path back to the Quay.

Medina's first sight of the '*Sea Hawk*' was one of delight.

She had often wished that she and her father could sail in one of the more expensive P & O liners which travelled down the Red Sea on the way to India.

She had never aspired, however, to anything so luxurious or which looked so attractive as the '*Sea Hawk*'.

She was aware as she went aboard with the Marquis that the seamen looked at her in surprise, but only out of the corners of their eyes, being too well-trained to stare openly.

The Saloon was a delight with its green walls and chintz curtains.

She thought it was a long time since she had enjoyed the comfort of a well-sprung Western armchair.

As soon as the Marquis came aboard the yacht began to move, travelling down the coast to the creek of which Salem had spoken.

When the '*Sea Hawk*' was at anchor, Medina, looking through a porthole, could see no houses and no people, only a vast amount of sand which was what she had expected.

It was then that she suggested to the Marquis that he should have something to eat as soon as dusk fell and before they rode back to Qana.

"There will be food for you with Salem Mahana, if you prefer," she assured him, "but this will be the last time you will eat Western dishes, and you may find it difficult to accustom yourself to our food which can become very monotonous on a long pilgrimage."

The Marquis laughed.

"I promise not to complain too often, and I hope, Ali, you will enjoy my Chef's culinary efforts because he is considered very good by English standards."

He spoke as if she would not understand about English food.

Medina longed to tell him that in her travels with her father they had eaten many different sorts of 'cuisine' and had both decided they preferred the French.

Dinner with the Marquis was served in the Saloon just as the sun was sinking in a blaze of glory and the first stars were appearing overhead.

Medina ate slowly in order to enjoy every mouthful. When the stewards had left the Saloon the Marquis said:

"I am looking forward to you telling me about yourself. I find it extraordinary that at your age, and you cannot be very old, you should be recommended with such a glowing report from Salem Mahana."

"There will be plenty of time to talk about myself

later," Medina replied evasively. "I see you have many books in that case. Have they been of some help to you?"

"A great help!" the Marquis replied, "And one in particular which was given to me by Richard Burton."

"I am a great admirer of Mr. Burton," Medina replied. "What book did he give to you?"

"It is called '*The Perfume of the Gods*'," the Marquis replied, "and is by a man I am hoping to meet while I am in Arabia, called Professor Edmund Tewin."

Medina drew in her breath.

This was something she had not expected, and it took her a moment before she could say:

"I have . . read the book of which . . you speak and . . found it very . . enjoyable."

"You read English?"

"Yes."

"Then it will be easier for me to talk about it," the Marquis said. "I find it one of the most exciting and unusual books I have ever read!"

Medina thought that was exactly what she had felt when she had read it herself.

She knew that her father had been more proud of it than any of the other books he had written.

"I suppose," the Marquis was saying, as if he was following his own thoughts, "I should not take it with me in case anyone thought it strange that an Arab trader should read English."

"If we are in danger of being searched, then you can say it is mine," Medina smiled.

"Then it shall certainly be in my luggage," the Marquis said firmly. "Is it time for us to change?"

Medina had the feeling he was anxious to start his journey. The first step was to sleep at Salem Mahana's house.

"Nur will be waiting for you in your cabin," Medina said, "and I should be grateful if Your Lordship would send him to me when you have finished with him."

"You are going to change too?" the Marquis asked in surprise.

"Salem will have told anyone in Qana who is curious," Medina replied, "that I am going on a cruise with you, and directing you to Oman, where you will dock at Sumhuram, a port in the frankincense area."

She made a gesture with her hand before she finished:

"Tomorrow morning, there will be two ordinary Arabs staying at Salem Mahana's house, but I doubt if anybody will be interested."

"And who am I supposed to be?" the Marquis asked.

"Your name is Abdul Murid," Medina answered, "and you are half-Arabian and half-Pathan, which, in fact, is the disguise Mr. Burton prefers."

"Then I can only hope that I am as successful as he is!" the Marquis replied, "And as he is quite certain I will not succeed in reaching Mecca, it is up to you to prove him wrong!"

"We can but try," Medina said, "with the goodwill of Allah."

The Marquis showed her the cabin which was next door to his own where she could change and she was waiting patiently until Nur could join her.

She was fascinated by the way in which the cabin had been furnished.

There was a dressing-table which fitted against one wall, cupboards and wardrobes that were obviously expensive in which the Marquis's guests could hang their clothes.

She appreciated the thick carpets on the floor, the softness of the bed, and the sheets that were edged with lace, as were the pillowcases.

She had the idea, and she was not wrong, that the cabin was intended for a lady and next to the Marquis's cabin, it was the most important one on the yacht.

She had no ideas how many beautiful women had slept in it and yet perceptively she sensed them.

It was as if she could see them, looking as her mother

had done when she was going out to dinner with her father.

They would be wearing low-necked evening gowns, their hair elegantly arranged on top of their heads and their hands covered by long kid gloves.

Then Medina remembered that that was how she would be expected to look if she returned to England, and shuddered.

She had been only a child when her father had taken her away after her mother's death but she had heard him talk so often of the boredom he suffered when he was with his relatives.

He described very eloquently the narrowness of their outlook and the way they disparaged anything that was new and different from what had been done for centuries.

And inevitably their violent disapproval of his way of life.

"How can I go back to England?" Medina asked herself despairingly.

For the moment at any rate, she was very content to be the son of an unknown Sheikh and the guide and teacher of a trader who was half-Arab and half-Pathan.

* * *

The cabin door opened and Nur came in.

"His Lordship is ready?" Medina enquired.

"He is ready."

Nur was an Arab of nearly forty who had been with her father ever since he had started his wanderings in Arabia.

He was, Medina thought, very much like the Nanny she had had as a child in that he looked after her, cosseted her, but at the same time was very firm in saying what she should not do.

He was always afraid that the camel-drivers might discover that she was not the boy she pretended to be.

Medina had grown so used to forgetting that she was

actually a woman that she automatically behaved as a young Arab would have done in the same situation.

Now she took off her grand clothes and put on the long striped shirt which reached almost to her ankles.

Her *burnous* was black, and her red silk head-cloth came down on either side of her face, held in place by two silk fillets.

As a concession to her supposed rank she stuck the bejewelled dagger into her wide sash.

Nur picked up the clothes she had discarded and placed them in the bag in which he had brought the other things aboard.

He opened the door and she saw that the Marquis was waiting for her just inside his own cabin.

He smiled at her appearance and she found it difficult not to tell him that he looked very distinguished and extremely handsome in his new disguise.

Nur had painted his face with henna and had accentuated his eye-brows and eye-lids with kohl.

He could easily, Medina thought, pass for an Arab.

Many of the tribes were exceedingly good-looking, in fact it was often said that their ancestors were Ancient Greeks.

They had either come to explore Arabia and been taken prisoner or else they had stayed because they liked the country.

Whatever the reason, amongst the tribes there were many different characteristics in their appearance.

Unless he spoke there would be no reason to suspect that the Marquis was anything but what he appeared to be.

"What do we do next?" he asked.

"We go ashore," Medina answered, "where the horses will be waiting for us."

The Marquis did not comment but merely led the way and they climbed down the side of the yacht, using a rope-ladder, into the small boat that was waiting.

Two sailors rowed them ashore.

The Marquis had already given his instructions to the Captain that, as soon as they had left, the yacht was to proceed up the coast.

Then in two weeks' time it was to be moved into the harbour at Aden to await his instructions.

He vaguely thought that, once he had entered Mecca, he would be able to send a messenger.

He would tell the Captain of the '*Sea Hawk*' to meet him at Jiddah or if that was too dangerous, Elat further North.

If both were impossible, then perhaps he would have to trek back to Qana.

He really did not know the answers and thought he must leave it to fate.

All that mattered was that the yacht should be there when he needed it, so that he could return to England.

There were three horses waiting for them: thin frisky little Arab beasts which Salem had sent to carry them to his house.

As they started off over the soft sand at quite a good pace the Marquis thought he was stepping from reality into dreamland.

It might turn out to be a nightmare, but for the moment he was content because he was in a different world from one he had ever known before.

He noted that Ali rode extremely well, and he wondered how the boy would fare if he ever came to England and he would certainly appreciate the superb horses which filled his stables.

All that concerned him at the moment however was that the young lad was really as good at his job as Salem had pronounced him to be.

The Marquis had actually expected somebody older who was not so well-bred.

He had told himself he would have the usual sort of guide that was to be found in any Eastern City and who took his percentage on every order he gave on behalf of his master.

But such guides were efficient, as the Marquis had proved to himself in India and other places in the Orient.

He had never for a moment envisaged that he would have anyone as young as Ali.

Or that the lad should have such a glowing recommendation from someone like Salem Mahana whom Richard Burton had told him to trust.

"I only hope he knows what he is doing," the Marquis said to himself as they rode on.

The stars filled the sky with an unbelievable brightness and it was easy to see their way.

It was on a sandy track which for thousands of years had been trodden by the camels carrying frankincense and myrrh to and from Oman.

There was no sign of anyone, man or beast.

There was the magic of the stars and the cool of the night.

When finally they saw the lights of Qana ahead, the Marquis was sorry their ride was over.

He wanted to go on and on, feeling the spirits of past civilizations encompassing him.

Then, just before they reached the first house in Qana he was conscious that while he had been riding he had become aware of something else.

For a moment he could not think what it was.

Then he knew that it was the strange pungent scent of incense.

Already he was on the Frankincense Trail which would carry him to Mecca.

He instinctively drew in his horse and only when it was walking did Medina do the same.

As she looked at him enquiringly and he saw the starlight glinting on her spectacles he said:

"To me this is the beginning of a great adventure, and I cannot help asking myself how it will end."

"I can only hope, My Lord, that it will bring you your heart's desire," Medina replied.

She spoke without thinking; then she realised they were both speaking in English.

"My heart's desire!" the Marquis repeated reflectively, "that is very unlikely. But at least I will travel optimistically and with hope."

"Then of course I can only say: '*Khayr Inshallah*'," Medina said.

"If Allah pleases!" the Marquis translated a little cynically, "But supposing He does not?"

"Then for you," Medina replied, "there is always the way back, and of course, England will be waiting for you."

She could not help there being just a touch of mockery in her voice.

Then as if she was afraid she had said too much, she touched her horse.

As it sprang forward, there was nothing the Marquis could do but follow her.

As he did so he thought it was a very strange thing for Ali to say.

He wondered how an Arab boy could be aware that England was waiting for him and if so — why?

Chapter Four

MEDINA AWOKE and knew she felt very much more rested and relaxed than she had been the day before.

At the same time, she was glad they were not leaving early in the morning as she knew the Marquis had expected.

When they arrived back, Salem Mahana had said to the Marquis:

"I hope you will not be disappointed, My Lord, but to get you the very best drivers and the fastest camels will take a longer time than I expected. I therefore suggest that you stay here in my house and study Arabic with Ali."

Medina knew as he spoke that he had found no reliable drivers as good as those with whom she had returned to Qana.

To use them again would mean a rest of at least three days.

She thought, because she knew the men so well and the animals were in fact the finest with whom she had journeyed for a long time, he was wise to make them wait.

She also thought it an excellent idea that the Marquis should study Arabic for longer than he had done already.

She had been surprised at the fluency with which he spoke, although she was well aware he had made a great number of mistakes which could later endanger his life.

She was thinking of how she should teach him when Nur came to call her.

"Everything all right!" he said in a tone of satisfaction. "English gentleman sleep on roof and in good temper."

Medina laughed.

She had wondered if the Marquis would avail himself of Salem Mahana's suggestion that as it was so hot, he should sleep on the roof rather than in the room that had been provided for him.

She knew it was usual for most Arabs to prefer sleeping on the roof.

But she had wondered if this was the first time that the Marquis had slept directly under the stars.

After she had eaten what Nur brought she dressed herself quickly, which was not difficult with the few clothes an Arab required.

She added the silk head-dress and her steel spectacles and went below.

Salem Mahana had apparently gone out and the Marquis was in the room in which he always sat.

He was wandering around it, looking at the strange things it contained and was, when Medina entered, admiring a votive offering which she knew came from a tomb at Al Jubah.

The Marquis turned round as she entered.

He was bareheaded and she thought again how handsome he was and how different from what she had expected.

"I am finding the contents of this room fascinating," he said in Arabic without a formal greeting.

"I thought you would," Medina replied, "but as an Arab you should have greeted me with the word: '*Salaam*'."

The Marquis laughed.

"I apologise, Teacher!" he said mockingly.

"It is important that you should never make a mistake even when we are alone," Medina said seriously. "I am sure Mr. Burton will have told you that one slip of the tongue, however small, one unwary gesture, can, when you reach Mecca, mean the difference between life and death."

"You are right, of course you are right," the Marquis said.

She thought perhaps it was an effort on his part to admit he was wrong to anyone who was obviously younger than himself and she said quickly:

"I suggest we start your lessons right away, and there is a place at the back of the house where we will be cool and get what breeze there is from the sea."

The Marquis in response made a typical Arab gesture as he said:

"I am in your hands."

Medina led the way to where, as she had said, there was a place almost like a verandah which looked out over a small garden. Beyond were the sands sweeping towards the sea.

The sun was very warm but they could sit in the shadow of the arched alcove.

As Salem must have anticipated that was where they would go, there was a low table between two soft cushions on a Persian carpet.

There was also a pile of books and a large quill pen, besides an inkpot made of sandstone.

Medina sat cross-legged on the carpet, pushing the cushion behind her back.

The Marquis attempted to do the same and because he took so much exercise, his legs were not as stiff as she would have expected.

He achieved the Eastern position, but not the Lotus one connected with the Buddha.

Medina knew perceptively that he was very pleased with himself, being able to copy her. She did not speak of it, but only started to talk to him in Arabic.

When he answered her, she corrected every word he pronounced wrongly.

They talked first of Arabia, and she found he knew a little more about the country than she had expected.

Only when they had talked for two hours did he suddenly ask:

"Have you ever been to England?"

Because there seemed to be no point in lying, and it was something Medina disliked doing, she answered him truthfully:

"A long time ago, when I was a child."

"I am surprised that you should have done so," the Marquis answered, "but what did you think of my country?"

"I was really too young to remember much about it," Medina replied evasively.

"But you have met Englishmen since, like Richard Burton," he suggested. "What do you think of him?"

"I think he hardly fits in with the category of being an Englishman," Medina replied. "He has always said that Arabic is really his language, and when he is here he thinks like an Arab and forgets he belongs to any other nation."

The Marquis smiled.

"That, I am sure, is really the secret behind a good disguise. What you have to do, Ali, is not only to make me speak like an Arab, but also to believe I am one."

"That would be impossible for you!" Medina answered.

"Why?" the Marquis asked sharply.

"Because although you may not admit it, England means a great deal to you, not only because of your position, but because you believe with all your heart that there is no better place in the whole world."

Medina was speaking as she would have spoken to her father.

She was using her perception and saying what she felt rather than what she thought the Marquis would have wanted her to think.

He looked at her in surprise, then he said:

"Perhaps you are right, but for the moment, having run away from England, I am trying to forget it."

"One can never escape from one's blood."

As she spoke she thought it was true.

Her blood was English too and although she wanted nothing more at the moment than to be an Arab and forget that England even existed, she knew it was impossible.

"How can you be so wise about things which really cannot concern you in your life?" the Marquis asked.

"They concern you," Medina answered, "I want you to think of yourself, and to become part of Arabia for as long as you are here."

She paused before she went on:

"You are an Arab, you speak Arabic, you are part of the Arab way of life and under the protection of Allah."

"I have brought a book with me," the Marquis said, "which tells me how a good Moslem should behave."

"Then read it! Learn too, because it is important, the prayers that every Moslem says when he enters Mecca."

She rose as she spoke to show him that for the moment their lesson was at an end.

As she walked away, the Marquis stared after her, thinking that Ali was the strangest young man he had ever met.

He appreciated the grace with which he moved and the litheness of his body which he sensed rather than saw under the disguising *burnous*.

Then as he looked out to sea he wondered what Rupert would think if he could see him now.

For a moment, a wave of homesickness swept over him.

He thought of his horses in his stables at Anglestone, of the comfort and luxury of the great rooms and the parties he might have been giving for a number of his friends.

Then, just as if he could see it all and there was a series of pictures before his eyes, he was aware of the fragrance of frankincense.

It was as if the Perfume of the Gods brought him a

different picture and evoked an entirely different emotion.

Once again he felt that inner excitement that he had known the previous day. It was the feeling that something was going to happen that had never happened to him before.

He wanted to capture and hold it closely in case it eluded him.

* * *

Salem Mahana joined them for a strange meal of Eastern dishes which were in fact, if unusual, extremely enjoyable.

With it they drank a fruit juice which was thirst-quenching, and, the Marquis thought, delicious and the meal finished inevitably with the mint tea which he had begun to like.

"This afternoon," Salem said, "Ali is taking you to buy more frankincense to add to that you have already bought in Oman."

The Marquis looked interested and he went on:

"Your explanation is that you could not get as much as you required in the Dhofar region, and you have asked me to supply you with what is missing from our own tree."

"That is something which I shall look forward to seeing," the Marquis said. "I really had no idea that frankincense actually came from a tree!"

* * *

An hour later he and Medina accompanied by Nur had ridden out of the town.

Nestling beneath the roses the Marquis saw for the first time the scrubby, unpretentious trees from which the incense came.

An old Bedouin met them and, when Medina explained what they needed, he took them into a grove.

The trees from a distance appeared to be like large bushes.

Above them soared the black volcanic 'Fortress of the Ravens', and in contrast, the leaves and small white-petalled flowers seemed very fragile.

To the Marquis's surprise, the Bedouin holding a spatula-like chisel chipped away the grey papery outer bark of a branch, smoothing a patch about the size of his dark hand.

As he watched, milk white tears welled up on the green wound.

With his bowl in his hand the Bedouin moved from tree to tree and the Marquis was aware that he was bringing in a harvest which had been unchanged for thousands of years.

"Some trees," Medina explained, "have been tapped three weeks earlier, and from these the Bedouin will collect handfuls of the precious ooze."

She stopped at a tree where the white tears had hardened into a translucent golden hue.

"This," she said quietly, "is pure frankincense."

The Marquis watched fascinated as the Bedouin went to a small fire that had been lit from the broken branches of the trees.

He scooped coals into a small clay censer sprinkled on it a few beads of the golden frankincense and held it out towards the Marquis.

The white smoke curling up into the air gave out a subtle aroma.

It reminded the Marquis of the prayer altars he had seen in foreign countries and had not then realised that it was frankincense that had perfumed the Church or the Mosque in which he had smelt it.

On Medina's instructions he ordered a large number of pounds of frankincense.

He then managed to seem suitably dismayed and disappointed when he was told he could have only half the amount he required.

As they rode back into Qana, he said to Medina;

"I feel I have learnt a lot and it seems extraordinary that I have lived for so long without realising until now how important incense has been to the world, as it still should be."

She looked at him for an explanation and he said:

"Incense raises the mind so that instinctively those who smell it pray to whatever God they worship."

He was thinking as he spoke of the incense that lingered in Catholic Churches, and of the joss-sticks burning in Buddhist Temples.

Although it seemed strange, he was aware now that he too had always associated incense with prayer.

When they arrived back at Salem Mahana's house, they told him what they had seen and what they had bought.

They dined before Sunset enjoying the tender meat of a young goat.

It was when the meal was over that Salem began to talk of the things which still lay undiscovered in Arabia.

Medina was aware that he was deliberately making the Marquis curious.

"In Timna which you will pass on your way North," Salem was saying, "there is an ancient trade which has survived for forty centuries."

"What can that be?" the Marquis enquired.

"It is indigo," Salem replied, "one of the luxury goods which travels North with the incense."

The Marquis looked surprised, and he explained:

"For many decades, dark blue indigo loin-cloths have been worn by a tribe of Bedouins who live in the South, who are called 'the Blue Men'."

"Did they really look blue?" the Marquis enquired.

"They claim," Salem replied, "that a mixture of indigo and sesame oil rubbed on their naked chests and legs keeps them warm, even in the winter, which can be very chilly in the highlands."

"How extraordinary!" the Marquis exclaimed. "Personally, I prefer to wear warm clothing!"

"So do I," Salem agreed, "but Ali will show you the indigo workshops where old men with blue beards soak and stir the crushed leaves to extract the dye."

He went on to talk of the many statues and carvings that were still to be discovered in Arabia.

The Marquis was listening intently.

"Are you telling me that there are statues like those which have been discovered in Greece?" he asked, "Or the Elgin Marbles which now rest in the British Museum?"

"We have even better examples of craftmanship," Salem answered boastfully, "but the difficulty is that the tribes where these priceless treasures are to be found guard them fiercely."

"With guns?" the Marquis enquired.

"Archaeologists or any other strangers attempting to steal them do so at their peril," Salem replied.

"Will we carry guns on our caravan?" the Marquis asked.

"Your drivers are all acknowledged shots," Salem answered.

Medina joined in:

"Near Tarim's South gate there is a half-buried stone inscription which proclaims the laws of the City in 200 B.C."

"It is still there?" the Marquis asked.

"I will show it to you," Medina promised, "and you will learn that law-breakers were punished by banishment, and dishonest merchants were fined 50 pieces of gold."

"Anything so interesting should be in a Museum," the Marquis remarked.

Salem laughed.

"You can try to take it with you, but I warn you, if you incur the wrath of the local inhabitants, they will be very aggressive!"

To interest the Marquis, Salem produced some ancient coins that had been discovered in the Hadramant.

"They were brought back on the incense caravans," he said.

He also showed the Marquis portraits in gold on necklaces and others on coins which must, he said, have been used by those travelling in the caravans.

The necklaces, the Marquis thought, were surprisingly beautiful considering they belonged to the 4th century.

"If you can find one yourself," Medina remarked, "you could take it home for some beautiful lady who has attracted your interest."

To her surprise, the Marquis stiffened.

"There is no beautiful lady in my life at the moment," he said harshly, "and I have no desire to find one!"

He spoke without thinking because they were the first words that came into his mind and when he had done so he thought perhaps he had been indiscreet.

Then he asked himself, what did it matter?

He was talking to two Arabs in the back of beyond and nothing he said could be repeated or, he was sure, remembered after he had gone.

"If I am being impertinent, My Lord, forgive me," Salem said, "but surely at your age, you should be married?"

"I will never marry!" the Marquis replied. "I have found that women are treacherous and untrustworthy. In England we have an old adage which says: 'Who travels fastest travels alone'!"

"But whither are you travelling?" Medina enquired.

"That is the question to which there is no answer," the Marquis replied, "and perhaps that is the reason I have been brought to Arabia – to find out where I am going."

He rose to his feet and stretched as he said:

"For the moment, I want to reach Mecca and after Mecca, where else?"

As he spoke Medina could feel the restlessness within his mind and could understand that it was the same feeling which had driven Richard Burton from one exploration to another.

It was, too, what had made it impossible for her father to stay in England.

They had to travel, but neither of them had known where or what was at the end of a journey.

She sensed that what the Marquis was feeling was making him, although that was not how he would have expressed it, unhappy.

"What you should do," she said in a quiet voice, "is to live from day to day. Tomorrow is always ahead and yesterday is behind. It is today that matters, and it would be a pity to miss any of it."

The Marquis turned to look at her.

"A wise philosophy," he said, "but thinking of tomorrow needs hope."

"There I agree with you," Salem said, "so let us go to bed with hope in our hearts that tomorrow we will reach Mecca. That, for each in his own different way, is the culmination of achievement for every man."

Medina smiled at him, but thought it unlikely that the Marquis would understand what he was implying.

To her surprise, she realised he did.

Making the obeisances of an Arab he said:

"Thank you, Salem Mahana, and I can only hope that I may reach my Mecca — wherever it may be."

* * *

It was early in the morning two days later, that Salem Mahana took leave of his guests.

He and Medina were alone before the Marquis came from his bedroom, where Nur had been putting the finishing touches to his *kohled* eye-brows and eye-lids.

"You must take good care of yourself, my child," Salem said. "I shall be anxious until you return safely."

"You know I will be careful," Medina answered, "and I am very grateful to you for sending me on this trip."

She gave a little sigh before she added:

"I wish I was travelling with Papa, but perhaps because

I have the responsibility of His Lordship on my hands, it will make his . . absence easier to . . bear."

"That is what I thought," Salem replied. "But remember at all times you are in the hands of Allah. He will not fail you."

"That is what I want to believe," Medina said, "but I am afraid of the . . future."

As she said the words she felt ashamed at admitting how apprehensive she was of what would happen to her when the Marquis had left.

The thought of returning to England was like a dark pall over her head.

She wondered if perhaps Salem would find her yet another job to do in Arabia; another traveller to guide.

She wanted to ask him if that was his intention, then thought it was imposing on his kindness.

Instead she said:

"You are the only friend I have in the whole world, and I am very grateful that we ever met and that Papa was so fond of you."

"Read your father's book," Salem replied, "and you will find the answer to your problems."

Medina suddenly gave a cry of horror.

"I forgot!" she cried, "I nearly forgot!"

"What did you forget?" Salem enquired.

"Papa's book! The one he had written on the Queen of Sheba! He had just finished it the night before he died. I brought it back with me. I meant to ask you to send it to his publishers."

"Of course I will do that," Salem agreed.

"I cannot think how I forgot it until now, except that I have tried to do what you want and concentrate on the Marquis rather than on my own problems."

"You must follow the advice you gave him," Salem said, "and live for today. Tomorrow will take care of itself, and if it does not, then when you return, we can think again."

Medina laughed, and it was a very pretty sound.

She ran to fetch the manuscript of her father's new book which was wrapped in white linen and had lain in a drawer of her bedroom ever since her luggage had arrived with the caravan.

For a moment she held it against her heart, and wished she did not have to part with it.

Her father had read her almost every word as he wrote it.

She wanted to read it again; to linger over it and hear his voice talking to her and know she was safe because she was with him.

Then she told herself she was being selfish.

There was so much in the book that would help other people.

Just as his book on the 'Incense of the Gods' had helped the Marquis and perhaps hundreds of others, this one would do the same.

She knew her father had put a lot of his thoughts and philosophy into his book on the Queen of Sheba.

She thought when they reached Saba, as the land was known, that perhaps it would inspire the Marquis.

She herself felt sure it was the most exciting and the most spiritual country she had ever seen.

With an effort she forced herself to take her father's manuscript to Salem Mahana and put it into his hands.

"You will make sure that there is no question of its being lost?" she asked anxiously.

"I will send one of my own people with it to Aden," Salem promised. "He will give it with a letter to the British Consul, who is a good man, and, from what your father told me, is one of his admirers."

"You will tell him that . . Papa is dead?" Medina asked.

"I will tell him that, and he will send the information to England. It is only right that your family, Medina, should know of his death."

"I suppose so," Medina conceded, "but you will not mention that I am with you?"

"No, unless you wish me to do so," Salem replied.

"No, no!" Medina cried. "For the moment, I am Ali and have no idea where Medina Tewin is to be found."

"Then we will leave it at that," Salem agreed.

Taking the manuscript, he put it almost reverently down on a table.

Medina knew it was in safe keeping.

* * *

An hour later a caravan of twelve camels, two dromedaries which were ridden by the Marquis and Medina, started slowly to move out of Qana.

The sun was creeping up the sky and sweeping away the last twinkling star of the night.

In the port several small ships were being unloaded, having crossed the Arabian Sea from India.

In the town a blacksmith was at his clay forge beginning to hammer red hot iron into grappling anchors, which was a welcome order from the large ship which had come into port during the night.

There were many goats being led out onto the hillside in charge of small boys who looked with interest at the caravan.

Medina had pointed out to the Marquis before they left the good points of the camels.

They were young, their legs seemed strong, and they were capable of carrying the heavy loads which were being piled onto their backs.

A number of the sacks contained the frankincense which the Marquis was supposed to have brought from Dhofar and those he had bought in Qana.

The dromedaries were made to kneel and Medina and the Marquis settled themselves comfortably in the wide saddles.

Then with a last farewell to Salem they were off, Medina leading the way along the sandy streets.

There was a cool breeze from the sea and the Marquis

tried not to think of the burning sun which would rise later.

He was conscious once again of the excitement that seemed to rise within him, almost like a tidal wave.

They were on the Trail which, if he followed it, would lead him from the Arabian Sea where he now was, to the Mediterranean.

It struck him that, of all the ambitions he had ever had, this was the greatest.

If he failed, then he would have failed himself in a deeper and more spiritual manner than the mere fact of being unable to enter Mecca.

He found himself thinking as an Arab would have done, '*Khayr Imshallah*' – 'it is well if Allah pleases'.

* * *

They spent that night camped in a quiet place, high up so it was not as hot as it would otherwise have been.

The Marquis was amused to note that the young Arab's tent was some distance above his, and he thought it was because Ali, as he believed Medina to be, was asserting his authority as the son of a Sheikh.

Perhaps he was making sure that he was not subservient or beneath the man who was paying for the caravan.

They dined well, because Nur had prepared their food and was, as Medina knew, extremely skilful even in the most primitive surroundings.

They also had brought with them some of the fresh, juicy and delicious fruit from Qana.

As they ate with Nur waiting on them they talked as any two people might do in any part of the world.

The Marquis was amazed that Ali knew so many places in Europe, especially Greece, which he had visited only once.

It was of course now connected in his mind with the use of frankincense.

Medina had made him laugh when she told him the story of Menecrates.

He was a Physician who had had the effrontery to compare himself with Zeus.

He had been effectively deflated by Philip of Macedon who had invited him to a banquet and while the other guests were given a sumptuous meal, the Physician was served with the food of the gods — a censer of incense!

She also told him that the procession connected with the god Artemis at Ephesus was headed by virgins bearing incense.

She described a procession where women were dressed as Victory with golden wings and behind them came, she quoted:

"Boys in purple tunics bearing frankincense and myrrh and saffron on gold dishes."

"It certainly sounds very luxurious," the Marquis remarked. "Do you not wish you had been born in those days?"

Medina shook her head.

"I am happy to have been born now, so that I can appreciate what the Ancient Greeks gave to the world by making people think."

The Marquis considered this for a moment, then said:

"I suppose that is what they did, but I never thought of it in that way. We had to learn Greek at School and I found it a bore, and it was only very much later that I was glad I had done so."

"My father always said that the Greeks did more for civilisation than any other people."

Medina had spoken without thinking and the Marquis asked:

"Tell me about your father. You have not mentioned him before."

She looked up at the sky.

"It is growing late," she said, "and I think we should sleep now. We will be leaving early in the morning while it is still cool."

The Marquis appreciated the skilful way in which the question had been evaded, and his eyes twinkled.

He wondered if, like himself, Ali had run away from his responsibilities or perhaps had left home after an argument.

He felt himself becoming curious about the youth who was so different from anybody he had met before.

He realised how knowledgeable Ali was about everything in Arabia, but what he had not expected him to know about was the Ancient Greeks, the Romans and the early Egyptians.

Then, cynically, he told himself that he expected the boy was only showing off, and sooner or later he would find his knowledge was merely superficial.

At the same time, it was intriguing that he should be accompanied on this journey by someone who was definitely well-educated.

Ali could speak of things he did not expect an ordinary Arab to know.

As he lay down on the mattress which Nur had arranged for him in his tent, he said to himself:

"Tomorrow I will make him tell me more about his private life, his parents and of course, if he has one, his wife."

He had the idea, but he was not sure, that the Arabs married very young and their first wives were chosen for them by their parents.

He was aware that a Moslem could have four wives and he was sure, although he could not say why, that Ali was a bachelor.

Then he thought that whatever the Arab boy was or was not like, it was not his business. All that mattered was that he should get him to Mecca without being discovered.

After that, he would go home.

Yet he could not help asking himself if that was what he really wanted.

At home, in two months' time, the Season would have started.

There would be Balls, Assemblies, Receptions and the

Prince of Wales would be asking for him. So would a number of beautiful women.

He could only hope that he had disposed of Hester.

At the same time, there would be other Hesters, beautiful, alluring, enticing, until they were in his arms and when he had made them his, he would find inevitably that they were like all the rest!

He knew then how quickly his interest could fade from a fire that burnt fiercely then died down until not even a glowing ember remained.

"What is the matter with me?" the Marquis asked angrily. "Why should I want more? Why should I be different from other men?"

He knew he was different in that he was experiencing what Napoleon had called 'Divine Discontent'.

He had so much; yet it was not enough, and was not only out of reach, but he could not name it.

"What do I want? What the devil do I want?" he enquired angrily in the darkness.

He got up and, because his tent seemed to be stifling him, he draped his *burnous* over his shoulders and moved outside.

Medina had chosen to camp a little way up the side of a bare rocky hill which seemed to emerge unaccountably out of the soft sand of a desert path which trailed away to the distant horizon.

Now the Marquis thought a pool of darkness lay beneath his feet while above the great arc of the sky was brilliant with stars.

He looked first upwards, then a little way to the left and saw outside a tent that was half the size of his own there was sitting, cross-legged, a lone figure.

He realised it was Ali, and without thinking he walked towards him, feeling that at this moment he needed companionship, somebody to talk to.

To his surprise however, when he was still a little distance from Ali's tent, the boy sprang to his feet and disappeared inside it.

The Marquis thought it strange, but he walked on until he reached the tent, expecting Ali to come out and greet him.

Instead, to his astonishment, he saw that the front had been let down and was fastened securely, as if against an invader.

For a moment, he hesitated as to whether to call out and tell Ali he was there.

Then he knew that the Arab was well aware of it, had seen him coming and was determined to preserve his privacy.

The Marquis stood looking at the closed tent.

Then as there was nothing he could do, he turned on his heel and went back the way he had come.

As he lay down again in his own tent he thought that Ali's behaviour was strange and certainly unfriendly.

They had said goodnight on the best of terms, but the Marquis wondered if in some way he had offended the young Arab.

Perhaps, he thought, it was just his way of saying that when he was 'off duty', he wished to be alone.

At the same time, it was another question he could not answer; another puzzle for which he had no explanation.

He lay awake for a long time before he finally went to sleep.

Chapter Five

MEDINA HEARD the Marquis move away from her tent and thought a little breathlessly that she had taken a great risk.

Because she could not sleep and felt in need of air, she had gone out of her tent with her head uncovered.

She had removed the *kohl* from her eyes and eyebrows because they felt sore.

She was aware that if the Marquis had seen her without her spectacles and wearing only a thin white shirt, he would have known that she was a woman.

"How can I have been so stupid?" she asked herself angrily.

She had thought he was tired and had expected him to sleep peacefully.

It was only because they were near Saba that thoughts of her father came crowding into her mind, and she wanted to cry.

Once again she was aware of how alone she was in the world.

Although she had travelled far more than most girls of her age, and had certainly met many strange and interesting people, she still felt alone.

At home in the house where her father and mother had

been so happy there had been her relatives at the Big House and friends and neighbours all around them.

She supposed by this time that she would have been entertained by a great number of people of her own age.

Instead of which she had met Sultans and Sheikhs, Anthropologists and Explorers like Richard Burton.

What was more, she had been able to talk to tribes all over Arabia in their different dialects and make herself understood.

Her father had taken her many times to Europe, Greece, Italy and had had a long holiday in Spain and stayed at various places.

'I suppose,' she thought with a wry little smile, 'I have had a cosmopolitan education which has left me a nomad, wandering around the world without roots and without a home.'

She was sensible enough to realise that sooner or later she would have to return to England.

For one thing, the money her father had left her would not last for ever and she knew that once the Consul in Aden had informed the newspapers he was dead, the money he received every year might be transferred to her.

But first her relatives would have to know where she was.

"What . . can I do? What can I . . do?" she asked.

She knew she was questioning not the Allah of the Arabs, but her father whom she felt was still near to her.

Finally she fell asleep.

Only when she awoke the next morning did she remember that the Marquis might have thought it strange that she had hidden herself away from him.

Because she was a little embarrassed, she busied herself giving orders to the drivers, and inspecting the camels, eating what Nur had prepared for breakfast only after the Marquis had finished.

She knew without him telling her so that, because he had realised it had a great importance in her eyes, he was looking forward to seeing Saba.

They had already spent nearly two weeks on visiting other towns, after leaving Qana.

The first had been Shabwah – once called Sabuta, capital of the Hadramant kings.

They had walked through sand-drifted streets of what had been one of the most powerful Cities in Arabia.

Medina had shown the Marquis the remains of a Temple which had been destroyed by fire in the 3rd century A.D.

She also told him that ivories, fresco panels and pillars inscribed with fierce griffins had been discovered in Shabwah.

She was sure there was a great deal more.

He had wanted to stop and investigate, but she had moved him away to Sayun where they found a mosque surrounded by strange bulbous tombs.

These were however by no means as spectacular as the Al Mohdar Mosque in Tarim, where Medina took him next.

This Mosque was 150 feet tall and had a mud-brick spire.

They listened to the Muezzin called from it:

"*Allahu Akbar! Allahu Akbar!*"

On the following day they moved on again but not before the Marquis had seen, as Salem had promised him, the indigo workshop where the dark blue loin-cloths were dyed.

Medina had the idea that the Marquis was not so interested in the indigo as in the half-buried stone inscriptions near it.

He did not have to tell her that he was thinking of what he could take home.

She could see it in the way his hands reached out to touch some fragment of ancient history.

He would look at the pottery and statues for sale in the streets, invariably finding them of no particular value.

He was only interested when she told him that small

figurines of camels were sometimes found dating from 1000 B.C.

He laughed when she told him that camels were domesticated by 1300 B.C. possibly because they gave milk.

"'The ships of the desert'," he remarked, "have certainly proved their worth since then."

"That is true," Medina replied, "and the camel provides the Arabs with milk, wool, meat and leather."

"It is a pity they are not better-looking!" the Marquis teased. "I must admit to preferring my racehorses who, of course, are of Arabian bloodstock!"

With difficulty Medina bit back a reply that she would like to see them.

She wondered a little wryly if he had ever thought of inviting an Arab to his house in England and was quite certain that such an idea had never crossed his mind.

Then they were on their way to Saba and into the country which had once been ruled over by the Queen of Sheba.

For some reason she could not understand, Medina knew that if he did not enjoy Saba as much as she did, she would be bitterly disappointed.

It was not surprising, considering that the capital Marib had been the Incense City where her father had deciphered hundreds of inscriptions.

They had stayed in Marib for nearly a year and had become very friendly with its people.

Edmund Tewin had studied the remains of the giant dam, and had shown Medina inscriptions which proved that in husbandry as a trade Saba had prospered.

She related what she had learnt now to the Marquis, telling him how King Solomon had despatched a bird – a 'hoopoe' – with an invitation to the famous Queen of Sheba.

"You will remember," she said, "that the Bible tells us that the Queen, whom I like to think was very beautiful, brought to the Hebrew King spices, much gold and precious stones."

"She must have been beautiful, living in such a beautiful country!" the Marquis replied.

Medina felt a warm feeling within her because she knew he had been moved by the town silhouetted against the rugged mountains.

When he first had seen it on their approach to Marib, he had drawn his dromedary to a standstill, and stared ahead.

She had known then, if she had not known it before, that he was very different from other Englishmen, and his whole being was deeply moved by the beauty he saw.

She felt too that the spirits which vibrated in the very air around them touched his soul.

They sat side by side on their dromedaries in silence until the caravan had passed them by.

Only then did Medina say quietly:

"The Koran reveals that Saba was a fair land but the people in it turned away from Allah."

"How could they have done that?" the Marquis asked.

"They were cursed for their stupidity," she said, "which perhaps happens to everyone if they repudiate their own God."

He did not reply, but she knew he was thinking of what she had said, as they rode on side by side.

They stayed that night outside the town, where the fields were cultivated with wheat and with lemon trees.

There were also beautiful striped and crested hoopoes, which Medina pointed out to the Marquis, saying:

"I have always believed they are the descendants of King Solomon's feathered messengers."

He smiled and watched the birds flitting through the foliage until dark, and they listened to the familiar 'hoopoe' call, that seemed somehow to have a message for them.

Next day the Marquis saw the limestone pillars from the

Temple of the Moon God Ilumquh, all eight silhouetted against the blue sky.

"The Temple to the Moon God was oval-shaped," Medina said.

She had the feeling that the Marquis was thinking of the Queen of Sheba, because she had captured his imagination.

Medina had a strange feeling within herself that was almost one of jealousy.

It was then she knew that, when the Marquis returned to England, she would never forget him.

It was a joy that she could not even express to herself to talk to someone so interesting, so intelligent and in so many ways like her father.

She watched every day the Marquis becoming more and more absorbed in the history of Arabia, and knew he was exactly as she thought a man should be.

He was strong, masculine and authoritative.

At the same time he was reaching out for something spiritual.

She knew now why she had felt so lonely the other night.

She had been thinking that, when their journey was over, there would be no one to talk to as she had been able to talk to the Marquis.

But to him she was just an Arab boy who had told him what he wanted to know, taught him the language in which he had become very proficient but still he did not think of her as a person.

To her he was a man! A man, although he did not know it, from the same country as herself.

She was aware, because she was using her instinct, that he had a depth of feeling and a perception which was very unusual.

She could not express to herself exactly what she felt for him.

But she watched him through her spectacles, feeling his handsome face engraved for ever in her mind.

It was with a feeling almost of desperation that she

realised the sands of time were running out, and that shortly he would leave her.

It might be because he was bored and wished to return to England, but it was far more likely that he would lose his life in trying to enter Mecca.

It was then as if a dagger was plunged into her breast Medina knew exactly what that would mean.

It was then she cried out from the very depths of her being:

"Not that, O God, not that!"

At that moment she knew, as if her father was telling her, exactly what she must do.

Here in Saba he had been on the brink of discovering a statue that he had heard was buried within the walls of the ancient City.

It was an archaeologist from India who had told him that he had seen in a dream a statue of the Queen of Sheba, who had been worshipped with frankincense and myrrh.

It flashed through Medina's mind that, if the Marquis found treasures like those he had spoken of in Greece, then he might be content to forget his wager to reach Mecca.

It would certainly justify his journey if he returned home with the spoils.

He would leave her, but he would be alive and anything would be better than to know that he had died through her incompetence.

There would be no possibility of his leaving if he was detected attempting to enter Mecca in disguise.

"I must save him! I must save him!" she said to herself.

She thought for a long time before she decided to tell the Marquis what he must do.

They had pitched their tents near where Medina had stayed with her father, outside the ruins of the ancient City.

There was a place below them where the camels could

rest and where there was water from which they could drink.

It was correct in an Arab land to eat before sunset and by the time they had finished the meal which Nur had produced, the sun was sinking low behind the mountains.

The sky was a crimson glory before it was replaced by the sable of the night.

It was very quiet, except for the camel-drivers talking as they smoked, and an occasional grunt from one of the camels.

The Marquis's eyes were on the mountains.

Medina knew instinctively that he was reaching out towards the spiritual ecstasy which her father had always felt when he was in Saba.

"I have something to say to you," she said in a low voice, speaking in English in case they might be overheard.

"I am listening," the Marquis replied, but he did not turn his head.

She felt again that strange pang of jealousy because he was immersed in private feelings.

For the moment she was only an Arab boy who was interrupting his train of thought.

"When I was here last," Medina said, "there was an Indian archaeologist who told me of a strange dream he had."

The Marquis was listening but not, she thought, with any particular interest.

"His dream showed him where a statue of Sheba is buried," Medina went on.

For the first time the Marquis seemed attentive and he asked:

"And you think it could still be there?"

"I know the exact spot he identified in his dream," Medina answered, "but he did not remove the statue."

"Why not?"

"He was taken ill and advised to go home."

Now the Marquis turned his face towards her.

"Are you suggesting," he asked, "that we might find the statue?"

"We shall have to be very careful," Medina replied, "because the people who live here are very possessive and have no wish for their treasures to belong to anybody but themselves."

"I can understand that."

"Archaeologists have already been driven away at gunpoint," Medina warned.

"Do you think we can avoid them?" the Marquis asked.

"We shall have to go alone," Medina replied, "and we can trust no one except for Nur."

The Marquis thought for a moment. Then he asked:

"How far is it from here?"

"It will take us about a quarter-of-an-hour to reach the spot where the Indian believed the statue was buried."

"Let us go!" the Marquis asked. Now he was smiling.

"You will require a spade," Medina said, "and we must be careful, very, very careful that nobody suspects what we are doing."

"We will therefore walk to exercise our legs," the Marquis said, taking over. "I know there is a spade among the equipment lying by my tent."

He rose without hurrying, stretched himself and sauntered over the sand towards his tent.

Medina drew in her breath.

She knew he had risen to the bait that she had held out to him.

She could only pray that her father had not been mistaken, or rather that he had not been deceived by the information he had been given by his Indian friend.

A few minutes later she heard the Marquis telling her in Arabic that he was going for a walk.

"I feel stiff after so much riding," he said.

Medina thought he had phrased the words well and no one listening to him would believe he had no Arab blood in his veins.

When he joined her she was aware that beneath his

burnous he was carrying a spade.

They walked over the rough ground of what had once been the great dam.

Then they climbed up onto the higher land on which the ancient City had been built.

Now there were only the broken walls, fallen towers and rubble where once there had been the capital of Saba.

The stars had come out overhead and the moonlight, while casting dark shadows, turned everything else to silver.

Medina moved without hesitation to where her father had been working when he died.

It was an agony to go back to the place where he had fallen, and she had known when she touched him that he was no longer breathing.

Yet, she was certain at this moment that it was he who had put into her mind a way by which she could save the Marquis.

They reached what was left of what once had been a Temple.

There was a fallen arch, broken pillars and cracked tiles which might once have been a floor.

A stump of a plinth which might have supported a statue on which were inscribed a few heiroglyphics gleamed in the starlight.

It was close to where Medina's father had been told to dig.

When she had fetched Nur to carry him away she had turned back to fill in the ground he had disturbed.

It would have been impossible, she knew, for anyone who might be aware of his death to ask the reason for it.

It was easy to point out the exact place where she had replaced the earth which had not been disturbed for thousands of years.

The Marquis took off his *burnous*, and his shirt was of silk as befitted his supposed rank.

She could see clearly how broad-shouldered, strong and masculine he was.

Then, before she told him where to dig, she looked around to be quite certain they were alone among the ruins, and there must be no 'Peeping Tom' or curious onlooker to talk of what they were doing.

It seemed safe, although the dark shadows were frightening and the light from the sky revealed everything around them.

"Here!" she whispered.

The Marquis put his spade into the dry earth.

She realised as he began to dig that he was very much stronger and quicker than her father.

In a very short time he was more than three feet down.

She was just about to think that the information they had been given was wrong when the Marquis's spade struck something hard.

He lay down on the ground, reaching into the hole.

Medina prayed that it was not just a large stone or the foundation of a building, instead of what they were seeking.

He seemed to be groping in the sand for a long time, but in fact it was only a few minutes before he reached further down and grasped something with both hands.

He brought whatever it was up to the surface.

It was then that Medina gave a stifled cry of excitement.

In the moonlight she could see very clearly that the Marquis was holding a statue which was black with age, and which appeared to be made of bronze.

It was of a woman holding incense in one hand and an oil-lamp in the other.

"You have . . found it! You . . have found . . it!" Medina whispered.

There was an expression of delight on the Marquis's face and he looked at the statue for a long moment before he handed it to Medina.

Then he groped again and a moment later was holding in his hands a necklace.

It too, was black, but Medina was sure that it would prove to be of gold.

It was not unlike, but was much more elaborate, than the necklaces which Salem had showed them.

The Marquis moved his hand once again round the hole.

There were now coins in it which Medina knew would tell them when the statue had been buried.

"I think that is all," the Marquis murmured, "and perhaps it would be a mistake to linger."

"Yes, of course," Medina replied in a whisper. "But first fill in the hole."

She knew as she spoke that it was something he had not thought of doing.

Quickly he replaced the earth he had disturbed, patting it down gently with the spade.

To make sure it was unnoticeable, he scattered a few small stones over the spot.

Then with a smile he said to Medina:

"We have to carry our loot as well as the spade and I am wondering if we should wrap it in your shirt or mine."

It struck Medina that if she was really the Arab boy she pretended to be she should offer the Marquis her shirt.

But as she hesitated, he laughed.

"All right. It is my statue, so I must therefore provide its shroud!"

He pulled off the long Arab garment which was more like a dress than an English shirt.

Now Medina could see how lithe and athletic his body was and that there was not an unnecessary ounce of flesh on it.

It made her shy but she could not help looking at him.

He was wearing long pantaloons and above them his skin was very white compared to an Arab's and she said quickly because she was afraid:

"Put on your *burnous*! If anybody should see you they would know you came from the West!"

The Marquis was amused by the nervousness in her voice, but he did as she suggested.

He then knelt on the ground to wrap the statue, the necklace and the coins in his discarded shirt.

"Do you think you can carry these while I manage the spade?" he asked. "It would be a mistake to leave it behind."

"Yes, of course," Medina replied.

The statue was less than two feet high, but it was heavy.

As she pressed it against her breast under her *burnous* Medina knew she would have to carry it with both hands.

The Marquis had the same difficulty with the spade.

"We must walk back casually," he said. "If we hurry or look excited, we might arouse the ghosts who still haunt the City!"

They were more likely to be living people who resented strangers, Medina thought, and she felt frightened.

It had seemed when they were going towards the ruins it had taken very little time.

Now, as they walked back, it seemed to take hours before they could climb once more up the hillside to where their tents were perched.

Medina was certain that the camel-drivers were watching them.

What was more, although they were not aware of it, there would be other people who would be curious.

At last, when Medina's arms were aching and she was terrified she might drop the statue, they reached the Marquis's tent.

"Go inside, Ali," he said. "I will ask Nur for some fruit juice. It is to be expected that we would be thirsty after our walk."

Medina did not answer.

She only moved into the tent which was large enough for her to stand as long as she bent her head.

There was also plenty of room for her to sit cross-legged on the floor and for the Marquis to do the same when he joined her.

She had put down the statue, but waited for him to unwrap it.

She was longing to look at it more closely and try to ascertain if it was really what she hoped it to be.

When Nur joined them with the drinks they were inspecting it.

It was undamaged and Medina was sure, because it was a woman with jewellery round her neck and round her wrists, that it depicted the Queen.

They showed Nur what they had found and Medina was aware that he had nearly said that her father had been right.

Quickly, to prevent him saying anything so revealing, she said:

"I have told His Lordship, Nur, how I was told of the place by an Indian Archaeologist who dreamt that was where a statue was hidden."

She knew Nur understood when he replied:

"Allah be praised, Master! It is a great find!"

When they were alone, the Marquis said with a note of elation in his voice that Medina had not heard before:

"I think this is one of the most exciting things I have ever done! It never struck me when I was coming to Arabia that I could be so fortunate as to take home something of such historic value!"

"You will keep it?"

"Most certainly!" he said. "It will stand in an honoured place in my house."

He touched the statue almost lovingly before he added:

"Of course I will notify the British Museum and anyone else who may be interested in what I have discovered."

He gave her a little smile:

"Actually, it was what *you* discovered, and of course, if you will allow me to keep the statue, I will reimburse you for whatever you think it is worth."

"I do not require your money, My Lord!" Medina said stiffly.

"Now you are making me feel uncomfortable," the Marquis protested, "and although I spoke of it as *my* find we found it together, but it would be a sacrilege to cut it in half!"

Medina laughed.

"Of course it would! But I am glad for you to have it; and when you go back to England, it will remind you of Arabia."

"*If* I get back to England!" the Marquis replied. "If however, I am discovered in Mecca, then of course, you must keep it as a souvenir."

Medina gave a cry.

"How can you say anything so horrible? Have you not thought that if you die, I may die too, being instrumental in taking you to the Holy City in disguise?"

"That is unlikely because you are an Arab," the Marquis replied. "Of course you must swear that you were deceived into believing that I was who I am pretending to be."

He bent over and looked at the statue that lay between them, rubbing it gently with his finger until he revealed a little brightness on it.

"It will be exciting to clean this!" he said.

"Leave it until you get back," Medina advised, "and whatever happens, no one in the caravan must have any idea what we are carrying."

"Nur can hide it in my luggage," the Marquis said. "You are quite certain you can trust him?"

"I have already trusted him with my life," Medina said, "and as you know, I have nothing more valuable."

"No, of course not," the Marquis agreed, "and now I am trusting him with mine."

Nur came back later with the bag in which he had packed some of the Marquis's personal belongings.

He wrapped up the statue, the necklace and the coins in a long woollen scarf of the type the Arab wore when it was very cold.

It was his own scarf in which the colours had faded into a dingy grey.

He put the parcel in the bottom of the bag and placed the Marquis's personal things on top of it.

"I will carry this on my camel, My Lord," he said, "otherwise it might seem surprisingly heavy."

"You must be very careful with it, Nur," Medina said.

"The sooner we leave, the better!" Nur replied. "My Master always said when he discovered anything:

"'Never linger long in the place of the crime!'"

Medina knew he was referring to her father, but only when he had left the tent did the Marquis ask:

"Nur referred to his late Master. Was he an Archaeologist?"

"I believe he was," Medina replied casually.

The Marquis, sitting cross-legged, looked at her in the light of a lantern and said:

"You spoke just now as if Nur had been with you for a long time. How did you find him? Your father is a Sheikh. Is Nur one of your tribe?"

"Tonight I can think of nothing but the treasure you have discovered," Medina answered. "How can we have been so lucky? So favoured by the gods?"

"That is what I too have been asking myself," the Marquis answered.

"What is important," Medina went on, "is that you should take it away, out of Arabia. You can trust Nur. He would never whisper that you had anything so priceless in your possession."

She paused for a moment before she said:

"If it was known the tribesmen will rise up against you and take it back, even if it meant killing you in order to do so!"

The Marquis looked at her in surprise.

"You are suggesting that I return to England immediately?"

"Now I think about it, it would be the sensible thing to do."

"And give up my journey to Mecca?"

"Is Mecca really so important?"

"It is to me!" he answered. "Dammit, I have said I will go there, and not all the statues in the world are going to make me break my word!"

Medina did not say anything.

She had been so certain that if she could offer him an alternative, he would see sense and return to England and not risk his life for no other reason than that he had made a wager.

Because she knew how dangerous what he intended would be, she felt frightened and gave a little shudder.

"Are you really afraid for me?" the Marquis asked.

"You are not an Arab . . so you do not . . understand how fanatical we are about Mecca."

There was a little silence before she went on:

"We . . believe that the . . presence of an . . interloper will pollute its sanctity. Anyone so foolhardy . . however brave he may be . . as to violate the most sacred place in the whole of the Moslem world must take . . the consequences."

But even as she spoke, Medina knew she had failed.

The Marquis's lips were set in a hard line.

She was aware that her opposition, her pleading, had only made him more determined than ever.

"I will go to Mecca if it kills me!" the Marquis vowed fiercely.

"That is exactly what it will do!" Medina snapped at him.

She got up as she spoke, and walked out of his tent towards her own

As she did so she knew she loved him.

Chapter Six

VERY EARLY in the morning, before anybody else was stirring, Medina slipped out of her tent and went to her father's grave.

She found it easily because, after he had been buried, she had piled a large number of stones on it.

It looked something like a Scottish Cairn.

The wind had blown the sand amongst the stones and it was impossible for any stranger to guess that they had been placed so recently.

She knelt down beside it and, because she felt even nearer to her father than she had before, she spoke to him.

"Help me . . Papa, help me to . . save the Marquis! You know it is . . crazy of him to go . . to Mecca . . and if he dies . . I will . . want to . . die too!"

She whispered the words beneath her breath.

Yet she felt she had cried them out aloud and the spirits of the ruined City, and those which lurked in the mountains were listening.

"I love him . . Papa, I love . . him with all . . my heart as you . . loved Mama . . and I cannot . . bear him to . . die."

The sheer intensity of her prayers brought the tears to her eyes and as they ran down her face she said again:

"I love him . . and I will never . . love any . . other man!"

Then the tears overcame her and she wept and as she bent her head she felt as if her father's hand touched her.

It was so real, and at the same time so comforting, that she thought everything that had happened since he had died had been a dream.

They were together as they had been before.

Then the moment passed and she knew his hand had left her head.

Yet she could have sworn that he was not far away, protecting her as he had done ever since she had been a child.

Unexpectedly, she found she was much happier than when she had walked out of her tent into the darkness.

She stood for a moment, wishing she had flowers and frankincense to leave beside the cairn.

Then she knew it would be a mistake to draw attention to it, in case the curious onlooker might dig in that particular spot in the hope of finding treasure.

"Allah be with you . . dearest Papa!" she whispered.

Then she started to run as quickly as she could back to the camp.

No one had noticed her absence and twenty minutes after she was safely inside her tent, she heard the drivers stir.

They talked amongst themselves and the camels grunted as they were made to rise to their feet.

Nur was in a hurry to get away and the breakfast with which he provided them was very scanty.

Medina thought the Marquis would be hungry long before it was time for luncheon.

Then she told herself with a little smile she was worrying about him quite unnecessarily.

He was perfectly capable of looking after himself when it came to his creature comforts.

As he came from his tent he was smiling and she knew

he was still excited at finding their treasure the previous night and anxious to continue the journey.

Because she loved him she longed once again to beg him to be content with what he had found and go home with it.

But she knew him well enough by now to know that anything she had to say would fall on deaf ears.

If he had made up his mind, nothing would change it.

She was sure not even the Queen of Sheba herself would have been able to persuade him.

They set off on their dromedaries and rode for two hours before the sun rose and it became hot.

Ahead of them were the mountains which bordered the North side of Saba and Medina knew it would be cooler when they reached them.

There was another hour's riding before they did so.

Then the bare stony volcanic rocks were in strange contrast to the fertilised plain where crops were grown on stepped-terraces.

There was a narrow pass between two high mountains which Medina knew would lead them towards Sadah which was on the direct route towards Mecca.

Because it was easier to ride in single-file she pushed her dromedary ahead to lead the way.

She looked back to see that the Marquis was just behind her, the camels following.

Then as she turned back, high up on the mountains on her right she saw a curve of smoke and the echoing crack of a matchlock.

For a moment she did not realise exactly what was happening.

There was another explosion and the dromedary on which she was riding suddenly collapsed.

She was thrown over its head in a somersault, and knew no more . . .

The Marquis, realising they were being attacked, pulled up his dromedary sharply and was aware as he did so that the camel-drivers had all reached for their rifles.

A moment later, even before he could get down to the ground, they were firing at their assailant.

He thought it was something he should do himself, but was concerned for the moment with Ali.

He ran forward and realised that the fallen dromedary's heart had been pierced by a bullet. The animal was dead.

Ali was sprawled in front of him, his arms outstretched as if he had tried to save himself.

He picked the boy up and looked round frantically.

He was aware that they were both easy targets for whoever was shooting at them from the top of the mountain.

Opposite, so that it was below their assailant, was what looked like a dark hole or perhaps a cave.

Even as another shot rang out he carried the unconscious boy across the stone path which might once have been the bed of a river.

Climbing a few feet he discovered when he got there that it was a cave.

There was more headroom that he had suspected and he could almost stand upright. By just bending down he was able to carry Ali inside.

He set his burden gently down on the sand, and saw as he did so that Ali's spectacles had been broken by the fall and the red head-cloth he always wore had been thrust back from his forehead.

His eyes were closed and the Marquis thought for one terrifying moment that he had been hit by the first bullet and was dead.

He pulled back Ali's *burnous* to feel his heart. Then he impatiently undid the buttons of his shirt and put his hand inside.

As he did so his hand cupped something warm, soft and curved and he stiffened in astonishment.

As if he could not believe what he had felt, he opened the shirt further and saw not only a small rose-tipped breast of a young woman, but also her skin.

It was dazzlingly white in the darkness of the cave and

for a moment he found it hard to credit what he was seeing.

Then, as he could feel Medina's heart beating, he heard somebody scrambling up the rocks and quickly rearranged the shirt.

"He been shot, Master?" Nur asked anxiously.

"No," the Marquis replied, "only knocked out by the fall."

"No more shooting, robbers driven away."

"Robbers?" the Marquis asked thinking of the treasures they had found last night.

"Bedouins in mountains attack caravans going to Mecca and steal what they carry, but now scared off."

"I hope so," the Marquis replied fervently.

He looked down at Medina and made up his mind.

"Where is the nearest Town?" he asked.

"Two miles, Master. Small place, but we rest there."

"Go ahead," the Marquis ordered, "and find a house where we can stay until Ali is well. Pay anything so that we can have it to ourselves, do you understand?"

"Understand, Master!"

The Marquis waited until Nur left him, then very gently buttoned Medina's shirt up to the neck.

He rearranged her head-cloth aware as he did so that her hair was not the dark of an Arab.

It was paler with soft lights in it, which in the West would be expected to go with a white skin.

"Why did she not tell me?" he asked as he carried her to his dromedary.

He saw as he did so that the saddle and everything on her animal had been removed, leaving the dead animal on the sand.

They set off again, the Marquis holding Medina in his arms.

She had been knocked completely unconscious by her fall, and he knew she would doubtless have concussion.

It was important while she was in this state that they

should be in more civilised surroundings than a tent in the desert.

He was obliged to move slowly and he also wished to keep close to the camels. There was always the chance the drivers might have other assailants.

It took them nearly two hours to reach the hamlet which lay in the centre of what appeared to be an arid desert.

When they reached the village, Nur was there to greet them and he led the Marquis to a small house.

It had the usual white walls and flat roof like all the other houses, but it appeared to be in good repair.

When the Marquis entered he could see that if sparsely furnished, it was clean.

"House belongs *Muezzin*, Master," Nur explained. "He good man, but very poor. When I offer him big money, he say he sleep in Mosque."

"That is good," the Marquis approved.

Carrying Medina in his arms he saw that beside the Sitting-Room there was a small bedroom.

It only had a native bed made of four pieces of wood and four legs, the centre filled in with rope webbing.

He knew that Nur could make it comfortable with the soft mattress they carried with them but until he could do so the Marquis laid Medina down on the carpet in the Sitting-Room.

Without waiting to be told, Nur knew what was required.

While he fetched it from the camels that had been pulled up outside the house, the Marquis looked down at Medina and wondered how he could have been so blind.

Without her disfiguring spectacles she looked very young and very fragile, at the same time quite obviously a woman.

It struck the Marquis how much Rupert would laugh at him for being deceived.

With his reputation for being constantly with beautiful

women it seemed extraordinary that he should have thought 'Ali' was a youth.

Now he saw there was something very feminine about her, not only in her exquisitely clear-cut features that had a Grecian look about them but also in the long fingers of her hands and the elegance of her feet with their high insteps.

It would make one of the best stories ever to be told in White's, he thought.

They would laugh themselves silly if they knew for nearly three weeks the Marquis of Anglestone, with his reputation of being a Roué, had been unable to penetrate the disguise of an 'Arab boy'.

"Who is she?" he asked.

It was something he intended to find out as quickly as possible.

Nur brought in the mattress that Medina had used in her tent and a soft pillow to accompany it.

The Marquis lifted her off the carpet of the Sitting-Room and carried her into the bedroom.

There he took away her red silk head-cloth and as her hair fell in soft waves on either side of her face he knew that Nur was watching him.

"I imagine there is no Physician in this desolate place," the Marquis said, "and if there was, he would be of little use."

"I look after young Master," Nur replied firmly.

"I suppose it is something you have done before," the Marquis remarked.

"Many years."

Without waiting for permission he went to Medina's side, felt her pulse and put his hand gently on her forehead.

"Asleep," he said. "I'll find herbs to help young Master."

It flashed through the Marquis's mind that he might give her something dangerous.

He knew there were stimulants grown in Saba which the wealthy inhabitants chewed to give them energy.

Then he was sure that Nur would not harm Medina, and as the older man read his thoughts he said quietly:

"With Allah's help all be well."

The Marquis wanted to say a little sarcastically that Allah might have saved her from being thrown from her dromedary.

Then he told himself it was in fact a miracle that no one had been killed other than one animal.

They had, proceeding in single file through that particular pass, been a sitting target for any robber hiding in the mountains above them.

He should, he thought, be on his knees, expressing his gratitude that they had all been saved.

He looked down at Medina and knew how relieved and grateful he was that she was alive.

Almost sharply he said to Nur.

"Go and prepare the herb of which you spoke. I also am hungry."

The Arab gave him a somewhat startled glance and hurried away.

When he had gone the Marquis very gently took off Medina's *burnous* and the light coat she wore underneath it.

Now, through the thin silk of her long shirt, he could see quite clearly the curve of her breasts and her narrow hips. He could also see the long and exquisitely rounded neck that had hitherto been hidden.

He removed her sandals, then gently covered her with the rug under which she had slept in her tent.

He put her hands with their long fingers outside it.

It flashed through his mind that with her eyes closed and her face raised towards the ceiling she might be lying on a tomb.

Once again he wanted to know that her heart was beating, but he told himself he must not touch her.

Instead as Nur had done, he felt her pulse, and it was reassuring.

Then he went to explore the house.

The Sitting-Room contained a volume of the Koran and there was no window but through an arched opening he could see a small garden.

It struck him that once again Rupert would be laughing to think of him setting up house with a mystery woman.

She had intrigued and stimulated his mind and led him to a treasure beyond price.

Yet, it had never crossed his mind that she was anything other than she pretended to be.

"I must be growing old!" the Marquis told himself, "If I am so senile as not to feel the vibrations of a woman!"

Then he knew it had been very intelligent of 'Ali' to deceive him so cleverly.

This was only one more example of her astute mind that had impressed the Marquis from the first moment of their acquaintance.

There were a thousand questions he wanted to ask, knowing he would never be content until he knew the answers.

If 'Ali' was not the son of Sheikh and not even an Arab, then how could an English girl know so much about the East?

How could she possibly have hoodwinked him and the camel-drivers who obeyed 'his' instructions?

She had also aroused no suspicions in anyone else with whom they had come in contact on the journey.

The exception was obviously Nur and the Marquis thought that was the clue! He was determined to tackle Nur at the first opportunity.

There were however a great many things to do first.

He discovered that the caravan was camping in a sandy waste near the *Muezzin*'s garden.

In fact he could see them from the windows of the house.

The Marquis then walked to the Mosque to find his host

and to thank him for his kindness in letting him have the house.

He realised that Nur had bribed him into being so generous.

Then when he saw the inside of the Mosque he knew that funds were badly needed and his tenancy would prove a Godsend.

There were fruit and vegetables for sale in the narrow street, and he was aware that he was looked at with excitement as visitors were rare and the owners of caravans reputedly rich.

He knew Nur would buy the most suitable food to eat, better than he could.

But he could not resist purchasing both frankincense and myrrh which were laid out in sacks on the paving stones.

There was also a variety of spices which he thought might amuse Medina when she could see them.

When he returned to the small house she was still lying exactly as he had left her.

He stayed for a long time in her room and only when Nur came to tell him that his food was ready did he move into the Sitting-Room.

Nur had prepared an excellent meal from what he had been able to purchase quickly and when he had finished the Marquis said quietly:

"I want to talk to you, and it is best that you tell me the truth!"

He saw a wary expression in the Arab's eyes and asked:

"What is the name of your Mistress with whom you have been for so many years?"

He knew it must be a question the man was expecting.

At the same time he had not decided what he would answer, and for a moment he stayed silent.

"You must be aware," the Marquis said, "that I am no longer deceived into thinking that my guide is a man. I am asking you therefore to be honest with me. I promise we will keep the secret between us, and no one else shall know of it."

Nur shuffled with his feet before he replied:

"Drivers think young Master man."

"They shall continue to think so," the Marquis said, "but you tell me the truth."

Nur looked worried, and again the Marquis asked softly:

"What is her real name?"

"Medina – Tewin – Master."

Nur spoke as if the words were dragged from him. The Marquis stared at him in astonishment.

"Tewin?" he questioned. "Is she then the daughter of Edmund Tewin?"

"Yes, Master."

"Then why is she not with him? Where is he at this moment?"

"He died, Master," Nur answered. "Buried outside Marib."

The Marquis drew in his breath.

So that was the answer to why Medina, if that was her name, was alone.

He supposed when he had asked for a trustworthy guide to take him to Mecca there would have been nobody else to fill the position at that particular moment.

Now he could understand why Medina had been so knowledgeable about everything that interested him.

How could she be anything else when her father had written *"The Perfume of the Gods"* and was a friend of Richard Burton?

It seemed extraordinary that the man whose book had inspired him, the one man he wanted to meet, should be dead.

In his place was his daughter, who was lying at this moment in the next room.

"When did Professor Tewin die?" the Marquis asked.

The Arab told him the date and he knew it was just before he had arrived in Qana.

Now he could understand why there were moments when he had known that the Arab boy who was his guide looked unhappy.

At first he had thought it was something he had said or done to upset him and he knew that some Arabs were very sensitive and easily disturbed, especially by foreigners.

Then he thought the reason was not himself, but some inner problem which was perturbing him.

He knew now of course that Medina had been missing her father.

The Marquis was sensitive enough to realise that many people, after the first shock of a death was over, suffered more acutely than at the actual moment it took place.

Because he had trained himself to be perceptive he had known that at times the vibrations coming from Medina had been those of an inner agony.

He told himself it was his imagination.

That he was being influenced by the country; by the strange spirituality about it he had not expected and the beauty that seemed to tug at his heart.

When Medina had been suffering, he only wished she could have trusted him so that he could have helped her.

Then he understood that that was something she could not have done because if she had revealed that she was a woman, their relationship might have been very different.

He knew only too well what most men and most women for that matter would expect, if they were alone in the middle of nowhere.

A world where what was called 'Western Civilisation' did not encroach.

He told himself it would have been very different being with Medina than with women like Hester with whom he had amused himself in England.

He knew without any shadow of a doubt that while she could talk to him as if she was a man and intrigue and astound him with her intelligence, as a woman she was very innocent and very ignorant.

The few things he had said casually as man to man which had come into his conversation without thought, she had not understood.

He now knew the reason why.

The Marquis had always enjoyed the unusual, unexpectedly he found himself in a position he had never envisaged in his wildest dreams.

Strangely enough, however, he was not quite sure what he could do about it.

By this time it was growing dark. He asked Nur if there was anything they should do for Medina.

"Her in hands of Allah," Nur replied. "When she wake, she no think right, still suffer in mind, but otherwise better."

"I want to believe that you know what you are talking about," the Marquis said, "but I suppose, as you say, we can only trust in Allah."

"Allah good," Nur said in Arabic.

The Marquis knew there was nothing else he could do.

* * *

The Marquis had his mattress moved from the small bedroom into the Sitting-Room.

There was only a thin curtain between him and Medina and he knew if she stirred in the night he would hear her.

"I stay with Mistress," Nur had suggested, but the Marquis had shaken his head.

"Sleep on the roof," he said, "and I will call you if she wakes."

He thought Nur wished to argue with him, but was too afraid to do so.

Instead he went up to the roof and the Marquis lay down on his mattress near an open window, but it was a little while before he slept.

He was thinking of Medina and he thought the name suited her.

He wanted to know why she had been given it, and so many other things about her.

It was only just before he fell asleep that he remembered that since Medina's accident, he had never given a thought to the statue he had found in Marib.

It would, he knew, when he returned to England, interest the whole archaeological world.

* * *

The Marquis was fast asleep when he was suddenly awoken by a voice and was instantly awake with the alertness of a man who had often in his life been used to danger.

He knew it was Medina who had spoken.

He rose and went into her room where he had left by the bed a lighted candle in case this should happen.

She was turning her head from side to side on the pillow and had thrown off the rug because she was hot.

Nur had left fruit juice with the herbs in it on a small wooden table in a corner of the room.

The Marquis poured some into a glass and going to the bed knelt down beside her.

He put his arms around her shoulders, lifted her head gently and held the glass to her lips.

For a moment she tried to move away from it and he said gently:

"You are thirsty. Drink, as I tell you to do."

She was not conscious, but as if the authority in his voice reached her she sipped a little of the juice before he took the glass away.

Then when he would have removed his arm from behind her neck she turned towards him and said in a rambling voice he could hardly hear:

"Help me . . Papa . . help me! If he . . goes to Mecca he will . . die . . and . . I will want to . . die too."

Her voice trembled as she said in an unmistakable tone of agony:

"I . . love him . . I . . love . . him!"

Listening, the Marquis was mesmerised into silence. It was almost as if he had been turned to stone.

Then he realised that tears were escaping from Medina's closed eyes, and running down her cheeks.

Very gently he wiped them away and after he had done so, he realised she had sunk again into the dreamless unconsciousness from which she had just awoken.

He could hardly believe what he had heard, and yet now he knew. It seemed incredible that Medina loved him.

He had been loved by so many women and he had always been aware of it from the way they looked at him and the way they tried to touch him.

Also he expressed it to himself, they vibrated towards him.

But it had never struck him that 'Ali' had shown any interest other than in the duties 'he' was carrying out as his guide and teacher.

He supposed the disfiguring spectacles had prevented him from seeing Medina's eyes which would have revealed her secret.

There had been nothing in his voice, which the Marquis realised now was very musical, to alert him.

How could he guess that the 'boy' who had seemed such an unusual Arab was in fact a very unusual young Englishwoman.

It was certainly a complexity he had not expected on his travels.

When eventually he returned to his own bedroom, he lay in the darkness thinking that nobody would ever believe him when he told them about this journey.

It was a journey into the unknown which had begun because Hester had tried to pressure him into marriage.

He had known that the only way he could save himself from her tenacious clutches was to run away.

Now there was another woman encroaching on him.

He told himself the sensible thing to do as soon as she was better, was send her back to Qana and go on alone.

Then it struck him that he would find it very difficult to get very far without her.

He could imagine nothing more boring than to plod slowly up the long, hot, exhausting miles which lay between where he was now and Mecca, alone.

"I want her with me!" he said defiantly to himself as if unseen forces were taking her away.

"But she is a woman - and you hate women!" an unknown voice told him.

"That is true, but she had not encroached on me before, so why should she do so now?"

"What you felt for her when you thought she was a man is very different from what you feel now!"

"Why should I feel different?"

He asked the question, then knew the answer.

Medina was a woman, and he would be waiting for her to show her love in one way or another.

Did he not know of the wiles, the blandishments, the enticements that every woman used when he was in their midst?

He had grown to expect the first move to come from them rather than himself.

He had grown used to the invitation in a woman's eyes, the provocative pout of their lips. The way their hands went out to touch him as if they were afraid he would escape.

"Dammit, is there no place in the world where there is not some accursed woman who will not leave me alone?"

Even as the question came to his mind he wanted to laugh at himself for being spoilt, besides cynical and disillusioned.

He remembered Hester.

He felt himself shudder at the excesses of their so-called love which he admitted now was nothing but lust.

Then as he lay looking up at the stars, the light pouring

from them, he knew that Medina, whether she was a man or a woman, was different.

He could not explain the difference, he only knew it was there.

That, as far as he was concerned, he would not run away from her or even be frightened of her; she would never do anything to harm him.

He did not know why he was so certain of this.

He just knew that it was an undeniable fact that was as true as that he was in Arabia with her and they were both English.

Because he could not quite understand where his thoughts were taking him, he rose and went back into the room next door.

She was lying just as he had left her, her face turned towards the ceiling, her hands were lying in front of her on the silk of her Arab shirt.

She looked at peace and there was a faint smile on her lips which had not been there before.

Lips, he realised now, that were perfectly moulded as if they came from one of the Greek statues in his house. He had always been exceedingly proud of them.

He stood looking at her, wondering if she had really said she loved him, or whether he had just imagined it.

Then he knew the only thing of which he was completely sure was that she was very unusual, very different from any woman he had ever known.

She would never hurt him, as he had been hurt in the past.

He was as sure of her as if she was an angel who had dropped down from the sky to protect him.

Then he told himself he was just bemused by the starlight which was making him think differently from the way he had thought before.

Women were women, and there was no logical reason for believing that Medina would be different.

Yet as he went back to his own bed, he knew that she was.

Chapter Seven

THE MARQUIS heard Medina moving about in her room just before dawn, but he did not go to her.

He was aware that she was drinking some of the fruit juice and herbs and after that, staggering a little as she crossed the room, she went back to bed.

When he talked to Nur the next day he understood that the herbs would keep her asleep until the concussion had passed and he thought it would be a mistake for him to interfere.

He went to look at Medina therefore only when she was asleep.

Her face was cuddled against the pillow, her hair fell nearly to her shoulders, and he wondered how he could have been so blind as to think she was anything but a woman.

Nur said she would be well enough to proceed in about three days.

The Marquis therefore busied himself with buying a new dromedary and he inspected at least a half-a-dozen before he found an animal he liked.

He also became friendly with the *Muezzin*.

He was an intelligent man who explained the various passages in the Koran which the Marquis had not understood before.

He also told him more about the history of Arabia, which he found exceedingly interesting.

When on the third day he was sleeping on the roof and Nur had taken his place downstairs, he woke with the dawn.

He thought that if they were to move in the cool of the day, it would be as soon as they had eaten.

He went down to the Sitting-Room and found that breakfast was ready, and as he waited Medina came through the curtain which hung over the entrance to her bedroom.

He thought if her face was not covered with henna she would have looked pale. It was thinner than it had been before and it made her eyes without their spectacles seem enormous.

She spoke to the Marquis in exactly the same way she had before.

He realised it was friendly but by no means intimate and he was aware that she did not know he had discovered her secret.

"I am sorry to have been such a nuisance," she said as she sat down on the floor with the low table between them.

"How do you feel?" the Marquis asked. "You are quite sure that travelling will not prove too much for you?"

"No, I am all right," Medina replied. "Nur has given me some of his special herbs which have always been efficacious in the past."

"You must not do too much," the Marquis insisted.

"I will try not to," she replied, "but we do have a long way to go."

"Only to Aden," he said quietly.

She stared at him in astonishment.

"To . . Aden?"

"I have changed my mind and given up the idea of going to Mecca."

He saw the sudden light that came into her eyes which he was aware was one of joy.

Then she looked away from him and said in a disinterested tone:

"If that is what you wish, I think you are . . wise."

"You told me it was a crazy idea to go to Mecca," the Marquis said, as if he was defending himself, "and now I have the statue I can go home without feeling embarrassed."

"Yes . . of course," Medina said in a low voice.

She did not say any more.

When they were outside, the Marquis showed her the dromedary he had bought and she commended him on his choice.

He insisted however that she rode the one on which he had been travelling because he knew it was easy to manage and he was afraid a younger animal might be too much for her.

There was nobody to see them off.

The Marquis had paid the *Muezzin* the day before a sum which had made him almost incoherent with gratitude.

Medina looked around the little house.

She thought if she had not been unconscious how exciting it would have been to be there alone with the Marquis.

He must never know what she felt about him.

She realised now she only had six or perhaps seven more days in his company and that she must make the most of them.

They set off slowly.

The first day the going was not hard and they made good progress. The Marquis however insisted upon stopping earlier than usual.

"We have done enough," he said to Medina when she questioned him.

They pitched their tents at a small oasis where there was water for the camels and palm trees as a protection overhead.

It was, Medina thought, very romantic.

She wondered what she would feel if the Marquis loved her as she loved him.

"He is so handsome," she told herself. "When he returns to England there will be dozens of beautiful women waiting for him and he will never think of me again."

Because she was afraid of him knowing what she felt she put a barrier of reserve between herself and the Marquis.

As he was aware that Medina loved him he expected there to be signs of it in the manner in which she looked at him and in a thousand different ways that women always revealed their feelings.

Instead of this, he felt she had withdrawn so that he could no longer reach her.

Her replies to what he said seemed to be automatic and without any emotion behind them.

On the third day he began to feel piqued.

On the fourth day he was bewildered and, if he was honest with himself, annoyed because he felt he had lost her interest.

Could she really have said she loved him?

Then for the first time it struck him that perhaps when he had thought she was speaking to her father of him she was referring to somebody else.

Yet that was impossible, and unless she had changed her mind, she loved him as she had said, with her whole heart and soul.

He watched her surreptitiously as they rode side by side, and thought her profile against the vivid blue of the sky was very beautiful.

He saw as before, that she had pulled her head-cloth low over her forehead and the sides of it concealed her neck and a great deal of her face.

Now he was watching the graceful movement of her hands and the soft movement of her lips.

He found himself wondering what he would feel if he

kissed her and was sure that her mouth would be very soft, sweet and innocent.

He was sure too that no other man had ever kissed her.

He found it increasingly difficult after they had retired to their tents not to go to hers to continue their conversation.

He told himself he was interested in her mind but he knew that he had never forgotten the beauty of her curved breasts or the whiteness of her skin.

Because he was thinking of Medina he hardly noticed the monotony of their long trek over the desert sand or the heat of the sun.

Still he knew she was out of reach!

On the day before they reached Aden he insisted on stopping earlier in the afternoon than usual.

Medina looked at him for an explanation and he said:

"Tomorrow we will be in Aden. I want to enjoy for the last time the infinity of the desert and later to watch the stars come out one by one."

Medina drew in her breath as she thought that was what she wanted to do with him.

It would be something to remember when he was gone and she was alone.

She realised that, when he left her at Aden, she would have to ride back to Qana.

There she would ask Salem Mahana once again whether she must go back to England or whether she could stay with him.

When the Marquis had left she was aware that she would be even more alone than she had been before, for she would not only have lost her father, but also her heart.

"I love him . . I love . . him!" she said over and over again in the darkness of her little tent.

She looked at him when he was not aware of it and thought he was not only the most handsome man she had ever seen, but also that he was very different from any man she had met before.

His breeding and his blood made him undeniably aristocratic.

Yet she also loved the sensitivity of his mind, his determination which was so very masculine, and his authority, which she respected.

She liked his self-control and the way that even when he was angry, he never lost his temper or raised his voice.

"Papa would have admired him," she told herself.

She wished she could tell the Marquis that the book which he said had inspired him and which was always in his tent had been written by her father.

The oasis at which the Marquis had stopped was even more romantic than the one they had enjoyed on the first night of their journey.

There were more palm trees, the well was deeper and the water was purer.

Even the camels seemed more content as they lay down, their drivers propping themselves against their recumbent bodies.

The Marquis and Medina were at the other end of the oasis out of sight of the caravan and divided from it by their tents which Nur had had erected in the centre of the palm trees.

Medina had taken off her *burnous*

She was standing beside the last of the trees looking out over the desert to where just over the horizon she knew Aden lay.

They had eaten early before the sun had set.

Now it was gradually sinking in a blaze of crimson and gold behind some low mountains.

As the Marquis came to stand beside her she said:

"It is . . so beautiful!"

"It will be difficult to forget."

"Do you . . want to . . forget it?" she asked.

He thought there was almost a wistful note in her voice.

"I shall remember this day all my life," the Marquis replied, "and of course – you!"

He knew a little tremor went through Medina and he

thought it was the first encouraging response he had had from her since they had started.

It was such a very little tremor.

Yet it seemed to him that it was part of himself, and he knew at that moment that he loved her.

He had fought against his feelings.

He had tried to convince himself that he could leave Arabia and return to England and take up his normal life without regrets.

Now he faced the truth that he could not leave Medina without leaving his own heart behind.

She was not looking at him, she had made no movement, her eyes were on the horizon.

But just as he was vividly conscious of her, he knew that she was conscious of him.

He did not move, but he felt as if his whole being went out to touch her.

"I have something to tell you," he said quickly.

"What . . is it?"

"It is something I think will surprise you."

She was listening and he went on:

"While you were unconscious, and because I had nothing else to do, I made Nur bring me the statue we found at Marib."

"You are . . pleased with . . it?"

"I cleaned it," the Marquis replied. "It is not brass, as we thought when I dug it out of the ground."

"Not brass?" Medina questioned.

"No, it is gold!"

She gave a little gasp and he said:

"The inscription on it will, I think, prove, it was part of the Royal collection, and I am convinced it will prove to be one of the most remarkable finds that has ever come from Arabia."

Medina gave a little cry before she said:

"Now I understand why you are returning home so quickly. If anyone . . knew what you carried . . every tribe in the . . vicinity would . . want to . . kill you!"

"I am not worried about that," the Marquis answered, "I was thinking that at least half of the statue belongs to you, if not the whole of it."

Medina laughed.

"You are very generous . . but it is . . yours . . You . . found it."

"On your instructions."

She did not speak and he added:

"I realise now that I have to thank your father."

Medina gave a start and turned to look at him.

"M-my . . father?" she stammered.

"I cannot imagine why you did not tell me," the Marquis went on, "that you are the daughter of the man whose book has meant more to me than any book I have ever read."

"H-how did you . . know who . . I am?"

"I knew you were a woman when I picked you up in my arms," the Marquis said quietly.

"I , , I am sorry . . but Salem knew I would . . guide you better than anybody else."

"There he was right," the Marquis agreed. "You have guided me, taught me . . and inspired me."

Again he felt a tremor go through her before she said in a very low tone:

"I am . . glad."

"You still have not answered my question," the Marquis persisted. "How can I divide the statue, which is both yours and mine?"

Again there was a pause before Medina said:

"I would . . like to . . think of it in a . . place of . . honour in your . . house in England."

"I think you should come to see it."

He was watching what he could see of her face, and he knew she was wondering if that was really an invitation before she said fiercely:

"I have no . . wish to . . return to England . . but I suppose it is . . something I must do at some time."

"I think we should go home together," the Marquis said.

Now she looked at him in sheer astonishment.

"Are you . . suggesting that I should . . come with you as . . your guest?" she asked after a moment.

"I have a better idea than that," the Marquis replied.

Her face was turned up to his, her eyes looking at him enquiringly.

There was a little twist to his lips as he said:

"I am asking you, my darling, to marry me!"

For a moment Medina seemed to be turned to stone.

Then as his arms went around her she made an inarticulate little murmur and hid her face against his shoulder.

He held her close, then very gently pulled her head-cloth away.

His hand moved over the softness of her hair, then as he felt her quiver against him, he put his fingers under her chin and turned her face up to his.

"I love you!" he said, "And I know you love me!"

His lips were on hers and they were just as he had expected; very soft, sweet and innocent.

At the same time, he knew that for Medina the Heavens had opened.

She was swept into an indescribable ecstasy — up into the sky towards the Divine.

He was aware that that was what she was feeling and what he felt too.

He knew that never in his whole life had there been a kiss that evoked such an ecstatic response within himself and an unbelievable rapture.

As he kissed Medina and went on kissing her he knew that he had found the Mecca that all men seek which is the spiritual perfection of love.

It was, in every way, completely different from any of the emotions he had known in the past.

Only when the Marquis felt that he and Medina had flown into the very heart of the sun did he raise his head.

He looked down at her and thought that no woman could look more radiant.

She had, too, a spiritual beauty which was something he had never seen on a woman's face before.

"I love you . . I love . . you!" Medina whispered.

"As I love you," the Marquis replied.

"Is it . . true? Can you really . . love me?"

"I never knew it was possible to love anybody so much, or to feel what I am feeling now."

Then he was kissing her again, kissing her until she felt they were joined not only with their bodies, but with their minds and their souls.

They were one, indivisibly for all time.

* * *

A little later, when the sun had sunk even lower, the Marquis drew Medina nearer the oasis where Nur had left them a rug on which there were two soft cushions.

They sat down side by side and the Marquis kept his arm around her as he said:

"I do not want you to be tired, my darling, for when we reach Aden we have a great deal to do."

She looked at him enquiringly and he said:

"We will be married at the British Consulate, but first I think we must find you some clothes."

Medina laughed.

"The Consul will certainly not expect your wife to look as I do now!"

"You look adorable, my precious. At the same time, I think the future Marchioness of Anglestone should look a little more feminine."

To his surprise Medina moved a little away from him.

"What is it?" he asked.

"You have . . asked me to be . . your . . wife,"

Medina said in a very small voice, "but . . perhaps you are . . making a mistake."

"A mistake?" the Marquis questioned.

"Here in . . the desert you are . . just a man," she said, "a very . . wonderful man whom I love and . . revere . . but outside . ."

She paused and the Marquis prompted gently:

"Outside?"

"I had forgotten that you were a Marquis and . . somebody of great importance. Your friends may . . think I am a rather . . strange choice, and then . . perhaps you will . . cease to . . love me."

The Marquis pulled her almost roughly to him.

"You are mine!" he said fiercely. "You are what I have always sought for and never thought to find. You are mine, my Mecca, and I would no more lose you than life itself!"

He thought as he spoke how she had said that if he died she would die too and he knew that was exactly what he was feeling.

Whatever anybody in England might or might not say, Medina was his, and he would never lose her.

Because it was impossible to put into words, he merely kissed her until she surrendered herself to the closeness of him.

He knew then that all she could think of was the ecstasy he gave her.

He gave her too a happiness that was as glorious as the stars now coming out in the Heavens above them.

Then finally, because the Marquis wanted to look after her and protect her, he sent Medina to bed.

He himself lay awake for a long time thinking he was the most fortunate man in the world.

He thought too that he would fight the whole of Society from the Queen downwards if they disparaged Medina as his wife.

It was then he realised that he knew very little about

her, except that her father was a brilliant and compelling author.

Because the Marquis was sensible he knew he would have to make a great many explanations to his family and his friends.

They would of course, ask why he had married an unknown girl of whom socially no one had ever heard.

He was determined that Medina should not be upset or in any way hurt.

He knew only too well how catty and unkind women like Hester could be.

They would try to find any way in which they could disparage Medina and make her feel that she had done something wrong in capturing him.

"I will protect her from all that," he told himself, "even if it means leaving England."

At the same time, he wanted to take Medina to Anglestone.

He wanted to see her moving around the great rooms, sleeping beside him and gracing the opposite end of his table when they had a party.

"If she can teach me Arabic, I can teach her to take her place as my wife," he vowed in the darkness.

At the same time, he knew he was secretly afraid not for himself but for Medina.

* * *

They reached Aden early the following afternoon and went at once to the Quay where the '*Sea Hawk*' was waiting.

Medina went aboard without her head-cloth, with her figure concealed by her *burnous*.

She looked strange, but in the seamen's eyes, she appeared to be a woman and the Marquis knew they would not suspect that she had travelled as a man.

Because he was aware that Medina was tired not only from the journey but because of the excitement of their being together and the rapture of their love, he sent her to bed.

She occupied the same cabin next to his that she had found so attractive when she first saw it.

Because she wanted to please him she tried to go to sleep and, after a little while, succeeded.

In the meantime, having bathed and changed his clothes, the Marquis went to the British Consulate.

He looked very English in his white yachting trousers and brass-buttoned blazer.

The Consul greeted him with pleasure, saying:

"When we saw your yacht in the harbour, My Lord, we knew you would turn up sooner or later and I am delighted to see you looking so well!"

The Marquis's eyes twinkled.

He realised that what appeared to be a heavy suntan was, in fact, the remains of the henna which he had not been able completely to remove.

"I am glad to be here," he replied, "and I need your help."

"You know I will do anything that is possible," the Consul replied, "but first I think you should receive the cable which is waiting for you."

The Consul handed it to the Marquis as he spoke and he tore open the envelope.

When he read what it contained he thought that was all he needed to complete his happiness.

The cable was dated a week earlier and read:

"*HESTER MARRIED THIS MORNING TO EARL OF DARNSHIRE. COME HOME. I MISS YOU. RUPERT.*"

The Marquis was well aware that the Earl of Darnshire was an old and very rich Peer who had already had two wives and several children.

Hester had chosen a father for her child who would

at least provide it with a position in the Social World as well as plenty of money.

It was a relief to know that he was free and there was now nothing to prevent him from returning to England with Medina.

He put the cable into his pocket and said to the Consul:

"The way in which I need your help is in arranging for my marriage to take place, Sir."

The Consul looked interested as he went on:

"I would also be exceedingly grateful if your wife could tell me how I can provide my bride, who is with me, with suitable clothes."

"Suitable clothes?" the Consul repeated.

"We have been travelling disguised as Arabs," the Marquis explained, "and my future wife's luggage was left behind at Qana."

"Now I understand," the Consul exclaimed, "and I am sure my wife would be delighted to help you. What you cannot buy in Aden I am sure she can provide."

"I am very grateful," the Marquis said.

"In the meantime," the Consul went on, "if you wish to be married tomorrow morning, I will send for my Chaplain who will perform the Service. My secretary will prepare the necessary documents."

"Thank you," replied the Marquis.

"May I ask the name of the lady to whom I am to proffer my good wishes?" the Consul enquired curiously.

"Her name is Medina Tewin," the Marquis replied, "and she is the daughter of Professor Edmund Tewin of whom you may have heard."

"My old friend!" the Consul cried, "And someone I shall miss sorely, having learnt of his death only a short time ago."

"I enjoyed his last book," the Marquis remarked.

"So did I!" the Consul agreed. "He was a brilliant man — absolutely brilliant! I do not know whether his daughter is aware of it, but her grandfather is also dead. It was in the English newspapers which arrived three days ago."

The Consul rose and shuffled through some editions of the '*Morning Post*' which were on a chair near to his desk.

He found what he was seeking, opened it, and brought it across the room to the Marquis.

"Here it is!" he said, "in the centre page. Lord Tewincliffe was a very distinguished man."

The Marquis stiffened in surprise, but he did not say anything as he took the paper from the Consul.

On the centre page of the '*Morning Post*', which was two weeks old, he read:

"*DEATH OF THE RT. HON. LORD TEWINCLIFFE*

It is with deep regret that we announce the death of the Rt. Hon. Lord Tewincliffe, Lord Lieutenant of Berkshire and a distinguished member at the Court of Her Majesty The Queen. In his 80th year, Lord Tewincliffe died after a short illness and will be deeply mourned by all who knew him. His heir is his eldest son, Colonel the Honourable Alfred Tewin, who commands the Household Brigade. His second son, the Honourable Edmund Tewin is a well-known Author and Archaeologist, who is at present thought to be in Arabia . . "

There was a little more about Lord Tewincliffe's career and a list of the many Societies of which he was President, but the Marquis could only stare at what he had already read.

He knew it was the answer to everything that had troubled him.

Even his family, fastidious as they were, and indeed the whole of Society, could not disparage Medina's antecedents when they knew she was the granddaughter of Lord Tewincliffe.

Now, as he thought of it, he had heard of the old man.

Yet he had no reason to connect him with the Edmund Tewin of whom Richard Burton had spoken so warmly.

The Marquis was aware that yet another obstacle had

been dispensed with and now all he had to do was to make Medina happy.

"I love her, and our love is the only thing which really matters," he told himself.

*   *   *

The Consul's wife was an extremely practical woman.

When she realised what was required, she put the wheels in motion.

The dressmaker from the best known shop in Aden was sent hurrying to the yacht with almost everything in stock.

Medina awoke to find her cabin filled with clothes of every sort and description.

The majority of them needed inches to be taken in around the waist.

However she was able to find enough gowns at least to make her appear respectable until they reached Europe.

She had, before she went to sleep, washed the henna and kohl from her face and eyes.

After soaking in a bath she had washed her hair so that it seemed to have new life in it.

When the Marquis saw her there were little lights amid the darkness which he thought very lovely.

What she loved about him was his generosity to Nur and also to the camel-drivers who had brought them to Aden.

To Nur he had given as a present the two dromedaries and also the cargo of frankincense and myrrh.

When the incense was sold, which would be easy in Aden, Medina knew it would bring him quite a large sum of money.

The Marquis gave all the drivers a large reward for their services and a written recommendation which they could show to any future trader who wished to employ them.

He and Medina had said good-bye to them all at the edge of the City.

Nur, who had fetched them a hired carriage to take them to the yacht, had been the last to say farewell.

"Goodbye, Nur!" Medina had said to him. "I can never thank you enough for all your kindness to my father and me."

"You safe, Mistress. Allah is great!"

"I know you will go back to Salem Mahana," Medina went on, "so will you tell him that I am to marry the Marquis, and that I am very happy?"

"*Ash shvkr i illah* — thanks to Allah!" Nur murmured, and he made Medina a deep obeisance.

"One day we will come back," Medina said softly, "and we will find you, Nur, wherever you may be."

She saw the pleasure in Nur's face.

She could not however help feeling a little sad as she thought that she was leaving him and her father behind.

Her father was in a lonely grave in Marib, but she knew it was where he would want to be.

She thought too that it was all due to him that she and the Marquis had found the gold statue, which, as she had hoped, prevented him from wishing to continue his journey to Mecca.

As if he read her thoughts, the Marquis said:

"Did you really think that once I knew you were a woman — my precious woman – I would take you into danger?"

"Is that really what made you decide to come to Aden?" Medina asked.

"Of course it was!" he replied. "And I have been afraid for you every inch of the way! From the moment you fell from your dromedary until now that you are on British soil!"

Medina laughed. Then she said:

"Oh, my darling, I was so afraid for . . you! I prayed and prayed that somehow you would change your mind and . . not go on to Mecca."

"I can think of no better way to have changed it," the Marquis replied.

As he spoke, his eyes were on her lips and she knew he wanted to kiss her.

On board the yacht they sat talking after dinner until it was late.

Then the Marquis drew Medina out onto the deck so that they could stand looking up at the stars.

"Our . . stars!" Medina said softly. "They have . . watched over . . us and kept us . . safe."

"Let us pray that they will do so for the rest of our lives," the Marquis said.

He spoke so seriously that she looked at him in surprise. Then she exclaimed:

"Only you could say something like that!"

"It is what you and your father have taught me to say," the Marquis replied. "When I get a little more used to it myself, I promise you I will be very proficient."

Medina laughed.

As he kissed her she knew he was very different from the man who had stepped ashore at Qana determined to reach Mecca because he had a wager!

"I love you . . I love . . you," she cried in her heart as he held her lips captive.

*   *   *

The next morning, dressed in a white gown that had a slight bustle, she looked very young and very ethereal.

The Marquis was seeing her for the first time as an Englishwoman.

The night before she had dined with him wearing an Eastern kaftan which was the only thing in the dressmaker's collection which fitted her properly and without alteration.

Now, with her hair arranged fashionably by a hairdresser who had been sent to the yacht by the Consul's wife, and wearing a Brussels lace veil, to the Marquis she looked perfect.

In fact, he thought she was so lovely that there would be no one in the whole of London to equal her.

She still appeared to a be a little suntanned, but he knew that long before they reached England it would have faded.

Her skin would then be the same as the whiteness which he knew lay beneath the cover of her gown.

The Consul's wife sent Medina a cream that was guaranteed to remove any traces of the sun.

But Nur had provided her with some plants that grew in the desert.

Mixed with lemon juice, Medina was sure that Nur's plants would be far more efffective.

Because she wanted the Marquis to admire her, she had gone to bed with her face covered with Nur's special preparations.

She felt sure in the morning there would be a difference.

The Marquis however was more concerned with the expression in her eyes which radiated happiness.

The movements of her lips told him without words how much she loved him.

She left the yacht in an extremely smart carriage with the Consul.

The Marquis went ahead to the Private Chapel where the British Chaplain was waiting for them.

The Consul took Medina up the aisle on his arm and at the Marquis's request, the only other witness was the Consul's wife.

Medina was sure, however, that her father and mother were with her.

She thought she and the Marquis were blessed not only by God to whom they prayed in the Chapel but also by Allah.

He had brought them through so many dangers and difficulties and had given them the love which was theirs for ever.

There was a champagne luncheon at the Consulate

after the ceremony and the Consul and his wife drank their health.

They then went back to the '*Sea Hawk*', and the Captain immediately put to sea.

"At last we are alone!" the Marquis said thankfully.

As soon as they were out of the harbour he took Medina below to his cabin.

To her delight she found it was filled with lilies which must have come from the Flower Market in Aden.

There was also the scent of frankincense.

She smiled at the Marquis and said:

"What else could we have in our bridal chamber? It is a scent, my darling, which I think will be with us all our lives."

He smiled before he added very softly:

"The perfume of the gods, and of you, my precious, because to me you are a goddess!"

Medina lifted her lips.

He removed the wreath she wore and the lace veil and threw them down on a chair.

Then with his lips on hers she felt him undoing her gown, and as it fell to the ground she felt shy and hid her face against him.

Lifting her up in his arms he carried her to the bed and laying her down pulled the sheet which was edged with lace, over her.

A moment later he was beside her.

He pulled her close against him and Medina could now feel the muscular body she had admired in Marib.

She felt a wild excitement run through her.

"I love . . you!" she whispered.

"As I love you, my precious wife," the Marquis said, "and now I want more than anything else to see again the beauty of your breasts as I saw them, after you had fallen from the dromedary."

He saw her eyes look up at him in astonishment, and he explained:

"That was when I learnt that you were not what you

pretended to be. I felt for your heart, thinking perhaps you were dead, and found something soft, white and exquisite that told me you were a woman!"

"I . . I wondered . . how you . . knew," Medina murmured.

The Marquis kissed her eyes, her straight little nose, then her lips.

He moved her hair to kiss the softness of her long neck, evoking within her sensations she had never known existed.

Then he was kissing her breasts; kissing them so that she quivered beneath him.

He knew that while he was trying to be very gentle he had ignited a little flame within her which complemented the fire within himself.

She aroused him and he desired her in a way he had never desired a woman before in the past.

They were seeking the spiritual, which they had both found in Arabia, and it would guide and inspire them all through their lives.

The Marquis went on kissing Medina, his hand was touching her and she felt that he carried her into a Heaven that was indescribable, it was so wonderful.

"We are one!" he said, and there was a note of triumph in his voice that was very moving. "We have reached Mecca, my darling. We have achieved the impossible and have become as gods."

Then as he made Medina his, they were swept into an ecstasy that was beyond words.

They knew that their love for each other was eternal.

Like the desert it would go on into infinity and beyond each horizon there would be another.

They themselves had become one with the greatest and most sacred mystery given to man, which is LOVE.